FIANCÉE FOR HIRE

A DOGWOOD SWEET ROMANTIC COMEDY
NOVELLA

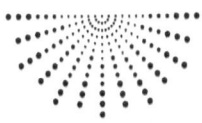

PAM MCCUTCHEON

PARKER
HAYDEN
MEDIA

ISBN: 978-1-950349-25-8 ebook
ISBN: 978-1-950349-28-9 print

Parker Hayden Media
5740 N. Carefree Circle, Ste 120-1
Colorado Springs, CO 80922

Art credits:
Cover Design: LB Hayden
Graphics:
Dog: adogslifephoto/DepositPhotos
Couple: deagreez1/DepositPhotos

CHAPTER ONE

THE DOCTOR'S diagnosis should have dismayed Logan Kelly, but he felt oddly relieved as he headed back to his hotel. Just the kick in the pants he needed to finalize the decision he'd been putting off.

But when he approached the hotel suite, he saw the lean form of his best friend and caddy, Ryan Nash, lounging outside the door. "Lost your key?" Logan asked with a smile.

"No, I just wanted to warn you about what's inside. Or rather, who."

Logan groaned. Not again. "Who is it this time?"

"Crystal."

Logan thought for a moment. Oh, yeah—the bleached blonde with the fake tan, big hair, and pink frosted lipstick. Some men found that look attractive, but he wasn't one of them. "How'd she get in?"

"How do they ever? Probably bribed a hotel employee or the dog walker. I asked her to leave, but she wouldn't go. And I figured you wouldn't want me to call security."

"You're right. I don't." He had enough publicity already

—he didn't need more of this kind. "How long has she been in there?"

"Not long," Ryan said. "I knew you'd be back soon."

With a nod, Logan said, "Want to help me get rid of her?"

Ryan grinned. "That's why I'm here. Ready to brave the lioness in your den?"

Logan sighed and closed his eyes for a moment. "Not really, but let's do this."

They entered, and found Crystal on her knees on the floor in his room, rear end up in the air, head under the bed. Logan assumed the low growl emanating from under the bed skirt came from his dog Mulligan, and not from the blonde.

"What are you doing in my room?" Logan demanded.

Crystal scrambled up as best she could in her short, tight skirt, and airily waved a chicken leg as she wobbled on her ridiculously high heels. "Just making friends with your cute little doggie."

Logan frowned. "How's that working for you?" he asked drily.

"Great," she chirped as Mulligan darted out from under the bed toward Logan.

The scruffy-looking terrier mix had dark reddish hair with the occasional white splotch and stood protectively by Logan, growling at the interloper.

Ignoring the dog's warning, Crystal smiled, tossed the chicken in the trash, and picked up a bottle from the bed. "I brought you this, to celebrate your win yesterday."

He was too tired of these kinds of confrontations to be polite. "I don't drink champagne, and I don't date women my dog doesn't like." And Mulligan rarely liked any of the groupies on the PGA tour, nicknamed the Party Groupie Association for a reason. "You know that." All the groupies did. Unfortunately, they took it as a challenge, and continually tried to win over his dog.

"Oh, she'll like me. All dogs do," Crystal assured him. "She just needs a little time."

"He."

"What?" she asked, looking confused.

"Mulligan is male, not female." Which she would have known if she'd bothered to look.

"Well, maybe he just doesn't like women at all. Did you ever think of that?" she shot back as if she'd scored a birdie.

"He likes my mother," Logan pointed out.

Before she could protest any more, Ryan took hold of her arm. "Time to go. You gave it your best shot, but Studley Do-Right here isn't interested in you, his dog doesn't like you, and you're breaking and entering."

Logan grimaced. He hated the nickname the groupies had bestowed on him. He didn't party and carouse like some other players, and was picky about who he associated with, but that didn't make him a prude. They were only interested in him because he was one of the PGA tour's highest ranking players, and had the reputation of being hard to get. Someday, he'd like to meet a woman who was interested in him for himself, and not his money, fame, or reputation.

Ryan continued, "That's three strikes. Yoooooou're out."

Logan quirked a grin at Ryan. "Baseball? Really?"

His friend shrugged. "Sorry, couldn't think of a good golf analogy. Three over par didn't have quite the same ring, you know?"

As Logan nodded in appreciation, Crystal pouted, saying, "But we could have so much fun."

"Sorry, you're not my type...or Mulligan's. Besides, I'm leaving the PGA tour, retiring from pro golfing."

"Yeah, right," she said. "At the height of your career? I don't think so."

"Come on, Crystal," Ryan said. "Or I really will call security."

"Oh, all right," she snapped, yanking her arm out of Ryan's hold. "I'll go. But some day you'll be sorry you turned *this* down." She skimmed her hands down her curves in case he didn't get the point, then sashayed toward the door with far more hip action than necessary.

"Wait a minute," Logan said.

She turned back in the open doorway, hand on hip, looking smug.

"Take your trash with you—chicken bones are bad for dogs." He dug the chicken leg out of the trash, slapped it in her hand, and shut the door in her shocked face. Wow. He couldn't believe how good that felt.

Logan sat down in one of the suite's comfortable chairs so Mulligan could jump in his lap. "Good boy," he told the dog as he scrubbed his ears. "You scared away the big, scary blonde."

"Retirement? Really? Did you think that would work?" Ryan asked as he plopped down in another chair. "You'd still have the money you won from the tournaments— that's what she's really after."

"I know. But I don't know what would stop her and the others."

"Maybe if you were off the market—married, or engaged."

"To who?" Logan asked in disbelief. With his schedule, he never had time to meet real women, and the only woman he'd ever even consider was off-limits.

Ryan shrugged. "I don't have anyone in mind, just saying that's the only thing that would stop her. It's better than that retirement ploy."

4

"It wasn't a ploy." Logan took a deep breath, then made the plunge. "I just made the decision—I'm retiring from the tour."

Ryan raised his eyebrows. "But you're only thirty."

"It's my shoulder. This last tournament made my rotator cuff much worse. The doc says if I continue golfing, I'll need surgery, but if I give it a rest for six to twelve months and get physical therapy, I might be able to heal without going under the knife."

"Either way, you could still come back to the tour after you heal. Lots of golfers have done that." With narrowed eyes, he asked, "What's really up?"

Logan should have known he couldn't fool his oldest and best friend. "I'm just tired of the whole thing," he admitted as he stroked Mulligan's ears. "Travelling all the time, fighting off the groupies, the whole party scene, being in a different city every week...." At first, the travel had been fun and he'd enjoyed the groupies' attention. But that had gotten old as soon as he realized they didn't really care about him. "I don't even know where we are now. Somewhere in Florida?"

Ryan nodded. "It's the Valspar Championship, in Palm Harbor."

"Well, the diagnosis was the final straw I need to say goodbye to this crazy life." He glanced at Ryan, knowing that his income depended on Logan's. "Of course, that means I won't need a caddy anymore. Sorry, buddy," he said with real regret. "I'll give you a great reference."

"Are you kidding?" Ryan asked. "I'm just as tired of this life as you are."

Logan gaped at him. "You never said anything."

Ryan punched him in the shoulder, softly, respecting his injury. "Hey, what are best friends for? I told you I'd caddy for you as long as you wanted to play, and I have.

You wouldn't believe the number of offers I've turned down to caddy for others."

Logan didn't know what to say to that. But he wasn't surprised others had tried to poach the best caddy on the tour. "Thanks, man."

"No problem. You're the only one I'd ever work for. Most of the others treat their caddies like servants. Besides, with the money I made working for you, I can afford to take it easy for a while, figure out what I really want to do in life. And if I'm no longer standing in your shadow, I might even meet someone special."

Logan grinned. "I could tell Crystal how much money you made."

Ryan held up his hands to ward him off. "Noooo, thank you."

"What *do* you want to do with your life?" Logan asked. They'd both lived and breathed golf since they were teenagers. Did Ryan even have other interests?

"I don't know yet, but it'll be fun to find out."

The last of Logan's worries melted away. If Ryan was cool with it, then this was the right decision.

"What are *you* going to do?" Ryan countered.

"I haven't thought that far ahead," Logan admitted. "I just want to go home for a while, stay with Mom and experience real life, give Mulligan more stability." Mom had room—he'd bought her a new house and a car with some of his winnings. He'd do more, since she didn't make much as a bookkeeper, but the stubborn woman refused, and still insisted on continuing to work for half the town of Dogwood, Colorado.

And though Dogwood was a smallish town, it still had doctors and physical therapists who could help with his shoulder. If he needed a specialist, he could always go to

Colorado Springs or Denver. Not to mention, Dogwood held the best memories of his life.

Longing for home, for stability, for community, suffused him. He'd missed it.

"Home—that sounds good," Ryan said. "But when you announce your retirement, you know the press will hound you for interviews."

"Yeah. You're right. I don't really want to do that to Mom." She liked her privacy, and she'd hate having her peaceful existence disrupted by a bunch of nosy reporters. "I can stay somewhere else. Maybe rent a room at the Lavender Cottage."

Ryan snorted. "Yeah, that is *so* you."

Okay, so the Victorian bed and breakfast was a little frilly. Logan shrugged. "After living in so many hotel rooms, I don't care where I lay my head so long as the bed is comfortable, and they agree to take dogs. The Harrington won't, but I know Lavender Cottage does."

"We can do better than that," Ryan said. "Come home with me. Dad has that big house and he says he and my sister just rattle around in it."

Wow, that sounds good, he thought wistfully. Just like old times, when they were teenagers and Logan had spent a ton of time at the Nashes'. Not only was Ryan his best friend, but his father, Tommy Nash, had been his coach. The only child of a single parent, Logan had loved the noise, bustle, and loving affection of the Nash household— Ryan's mom, dad, brother, and sister had been like a second family.

Now, of course, Ryan's mom had passed, and his younger brother had joined the air force, but it would still feel like home—something Logan really needed right now. "You sure?" he asked. "Maybe you should ask your dad. If the press finds me there, they're liable to show up on his doorstep."

"Yeah, right," Ryan scoffed. "As if Dad ever gets tired of telling everyone he coached the famous Logan Kelly. He'll bend their ear so much about his protege, they'll run screaming from the house."

Logan grinned. Ryan wasn't wrong. He glanced down at his sleeping terrier, blissed out on his lap.

"And before you ask about Mulligan, he'll be fine as well. Our last dog just passed, and Dad's been waiting to get another one."

"What about Taylor? How will your sister feel about reporters—and me—invading your family home?"

With a wave of his hand, Ryan dismissed that concern. "Oh, you know Taylor. She'll have no problem kicking nosy reporters out of the house. She's small, but she's mighty, and very protective. Kind of like Mulligan."

"Yeah, she's growled at me a few times."

Chuckling, Ryan said, "I'm surprised. She always had a crush on you."

He'd kind of suspected that, but since she was two years younger than them, he'd mostly thought of her as Ryan's little sister—a little bratty at times, but cute and feisty. As she'd grown into an attractive and alluring woman, he'd been tempted to see if there was anything between them, but never followed through out of courtesy to her two protective brothers. He shrugged. "She's grown out of that, right?"

Ryan made a dismissive gesture. "I guess. She never mentions you anymore."

That's what he figured. It was for the best. All he wanted was a chance to decompress in peace, relax, and figure out what to do with the rest of his life.

CHAPTER TWO

TAYLOR NASH BUSTLED around Bar Pietro, taking orders, delivering food, and chatting with the customers. She gave Adam Diaz, the manager and bartender, the drink order for table five and paused for a moment to rest her weary feet.

"What are you doing working the bar?" Adam asked.

She grimaced. Adam knew how much she hated dealing with drunken passes. It wasn't worth the extra tips. "Solange called in sick, so Beth asked me to fill in for her." She'd hoped it was an April Fool's joke, but no luck. Double shifts weren't fun, but they did bring in some extra cash.

"Anyone giving you any problems tonight?"

Taylor glanced at table six, where four office monkeys were celebrating one guy's promotion and enjoying happy hour a bit too much. "Maybe."

"Well, if they do, let me know and I'll take care of it. Beth has no problem with me eighty-sixing any troublemakers."

Taylor grinned. Adam could, too—tall, broad, and built like a Mack truck, he could intimidate any number of drunks. But Beth wouldn't care for them causing a scene in her place if they could help it. Best to nip this in the bud before it turned into something nasty. "Thanks. I appreciate it. I'm cutting them off."

She delivered the drinks to table four and took checks to the guys at table six who were laughing uproariously at something.

One of them, a geek with glasses and a loosened tie, said, "Hey, baby. Want to have some fun?" and slipped his arm around her waist.

She removed his arm, and placed it firmly back on the table. "I'm not on the menu."

"Well, you should be," he said. "A little bitty thing like you would make a great appetizer."

The other guys guffawed. Wishing she could punch him in his stupid face, she said through clenched teeth, "Here's your check. You're cut off. You can pay here at the table."

She started to turn away, but he grabbed her by the wrist. "No, baby. Stay with us. Help me celebrate."

Glaring at him, she said, "Let go or the manager will make sure you do."

They glanced over at Adam who gave them a death stare. The geek released her. "Oh, now why you gotta do that?"

"Is there a problem here?" someone asked from behind her.

She recognized that voice and turned to see Ryan...and Logan. Her heart leapt. Dealing with drunks didn't produce this surge of adrenaline—it was all Logan. He'd always affected her this way, ever since she was a little girl. Tall, with tousled brown hair lightened by the sun and a devastating smile, he made her heart flutter every time she saw him. Stupid heart. It didn't know what was good for it —and it was definitely not wunderkind Logan Kelly. Like always, she fought it back, and smiled at Ryan.

"Gentlemen, meet my brother and his best friend." Ryan and Logan both stared at the drunks like deadly gunslingers daring the others to draw first.

The geek who had grabbed her swallowed hard and raised his hands. "No problem here," he said.

"Good," Ryan said. "I suggest you finish those drinks, pay your tab, and head home real quick like."

Logan nodded, looking more menacing than she'd ever seen him. The similarity to an old-time Western almost had her giggling.

"Uh, sure," the geek said, giving her a belligerent glare. Luckily, they were still in the hilarity-drunk stage and hadn't progressed to belligerent-drunk yet. Not that the spindly office monkeys could win any kind of confrontation. They quickly gave their credit cards to Taylor.

"Have a seat," she told her rescuers, motioning to a nearby table. "Two drafts?"

Ryan nodded, and she took the credit cards to the register to ring out table six. She didn't even care if they tipped her or not, so long as they left. She delivered the credit card slips to the office drones and the beers to her brother's table, carefully not looking at Logan. That stupid flutter happened anyway. But she didn't let it show. She *never* let it show.

"Thanks for that," she told her brother and Logan.

"Does this happen often?" Ryan asked with a frown.

"Only when I have to work the bar. Beth usually lets me work the restaurant side, but the bar waitress called in sick." She shrugged. "Whatcha gonna do?"

"Quit?" Logan suggested.

"Sorry, no can do. Some of us have to work for a living."

"Ouch," Ryan said, and Logan clutched his chest as if wounded.

Ignoring their theatrics, Taylor asked, "Did you want to order something to eat, too?"

Ryan nodded. "Two of your famous Italian subs with the works."

"Yeah," Logan said with a grin. "We missed them while we were away."

"You got it," Taylor said and went back to pick up table six's signed credit slips. The office monkeys had left without incident. The geek with the grabby hands didn't tip her at all, but the other three had more than made up for it. She took it as an apology for their friend's behavior.

She put Ryan and Logan's order in, then noticed Lana Henderson had finished her meal. She rang her up at the bar, and took out her brush pen to write in her best hand-lettered script: THANK YOU, TAYLOR.

Adam paused in wiping down the bar. "You don't have to do that for everyone, you know."

"I know," she said with a smile. "And I didn't for those creeps. But I like to keep in practice, and the customers seem to like it."

She took the check to Lana's table. Lana glanced at the check. "Your lettering is absolutely beautiful, as always. Have you thought any more about doing the Blake and Hewitt wedding?"

Lana, of Great Expectations Event Planning, now ran the bridal shop, and had been urging Taylor to use her hand-lettering skills for the many weddings in Dogwood. Unfortunately, it wasn't just a matter of writing out the invitations—they also wanted signs, seating charts, place cards, the works.

Taylor shook her head. "Oh, you know I'd love to, but with working here and taking care of my dad, I'm afraid I couldn't commit to delivering everything on time."

"Are you sure? It could get you in the door with a lot of other clients. Our busiest season is coming up, and you know I'd have a lot of work for you. Isn't that what you've been wanting to do?"

Lana had no idea how much Taylor longed to quit this dead-end waitressing job and do something creative and fun. Unfortunately, it took money and time to start a small business, and there was no guarantee it would succeed or bring her the kind of stability she needed. She'd tried to start it on the side, with lettering signs for the bar and other businesses around town, but her time was not her own, and she couldn't dedicate enough of it to get a business started. In maybe a year or so, she would have saved up enough to quit and try it on her own. "I'm sorry, I just can't right now."

Lana sighed. "Well, if you change your mind, let me know." When Taylor nodded, she added, "I hear your brother is back in town. Must be nice to have him around."

"It is, but I haven't seen much of him this week. Revisiting his old haunts, I think."

"And Logan Kelly is staying with you as well?"

The town grapevine was still as good as ever. "Yep. Haven't seen much of him either." Thank heavens. She didn't think she could survive being around him so much, though she adored his little dog. She'd taken Mulligan's standoffishness as a personal challenge, and was determined to win him over.

"Tell them I said hello, will you?"

"Of course. Though they're on the other side of the bar if you want to do it in person."

"Oh no," Lana assured her. "I'm sure they have enough people bothering them as it is."

That's for sure. Who knew golfers would draw such attention?

A customer at end of the bar raised his empty beer glass in a silent request, and Taylor nodded. "Gotta go. See you later."

"Sure. Keep my offer in mind, will you?"

"Will do." Not that it was ever far from her mind. But with taking care of Dad, the house, and working at Bar Pietro, she didn't know how she could fit it in. She was lucky to be able to practice calligraphy on her days off, not that she had many of those.

She delivered another beer, then noticed a commotion at the other end of the bar. She glanced in that direction, hoping the office monkeys hadn't returned. No, but there were two people trying to talk to Logan, whose mouth had firmed in a straight line. Ryan stood protectively in front of his best friend, his arms out as if trying to run interference.

Didn't look good for the two people, whoever they were. The guy was probably that same reporter who had been trying to get an interview at their house. She didn't know the blonde who stood beside him, flaunting her bodacious bod at Logan. Taylor sighed. *Not my circus. Not my monkeys.*

She headed to the kitchen where she found that Ryan and Logan's orders were up. Well, shoot. Now she had no choice but to head into that mess. She maneuvered around the strident blonde and the determined reporter to place the subs on the table.

"Crystal," Ryan said. "Can't you get it through your thick head? He's not interested in you."

"Oh, he'll change his mind," Crystal said confidently, winking at the reporter. "He's not married yet. Not even engaged."

Taylor glanced up and caught Logan's gaze, rolling her eyes. Couldn't the woman tell he wasn't interested? Taylor had gotten the message long ago.

Logan's eyes widened and his expression practically shouted "Eureka!" as he grabbed her around the waist. What? Not him, too. He'd only had one beer.

"Please, play along," he whispered, sounding desperate. Then, aloud, he declared, "Oh, yes I am. Meet my fiancée, Taylor."

"The waitress?" Crystal said. "I don't believe you." But the reporter gleefully recorded every word.

Ryan, the idiot, looked amused. "That's my sister you're talking about. And they've known each other all their lives. What could be more natural?" Turning to the reporter, he said, "There's your story—Logan Kelly returns to his hometown to marry his childhood sweetheart and retire. She wouldn't agree until he quit the PGA tour."

Taylor stayed frozen in surprise and hormonal shock as her brother spun out the story, the reporter lapping it up eagerly. Logan leaned in as if to nuzzle her ear and whispered, "Please play along—I'll make it worth your while."

The feel of Logan's breath on her neck was enough to make anyone flutter and melt. And she was no exception. But how could she "play along"? She'd fought her feelings for him all her life since it was obvious he'd never see her as anything else but a little sister. This was no time to let her guard down.

Then again, they'd helped her earlier, and she didn't want to call them liars or let the reporter and the annoying blonde get what they wanted.

That decided her. She softened against him and put her arms around his neck, smiling as if he were her moon and stars. "Yes, we're engaged," she said loud enough for the interlopers to hear.

Then she leaned in and whispered, "But it's gonna cost you."

CHAPTER THREE

ALMOST IMMEDIATELY, Logan regretted his impulsive action. What the heck was he thinking? The plain truth was, he hadn't been thinking at all. Sick and tired of fighting off Crystal and her ilk, he'd remembered that Ryan had said the only thing that would stop them was his engagement, so he'd panicked and leapt on the first available female he could trust—Taylor. He held the diminutive firecracker in his arms, gingerly, afraid she'd explode in his face.

Now he was evidently going to have to pay the price—whatever she wanted.

"Ha," Crystal said. "I don't believe you. You're just trying to make me jealous."

"No," Logan said with all sincerity. "I'm really not."

She brightened. "Wait—I just remembered the date. This is an April Fool's Day joke, isn't it?"

He felt Taylor stiffen. No, no, he didn't want her to think this was a joke on her. "No," he said firmly. "The date is a bad coincidence. I'll tell you the same thing tomorrow."

"That's right," Ryan said. "Joking about marriage would

be very wrong. This is real." He spoke more to Taylor than to Crystal, and Logan felt Taylor relax.

"If you're engaged, then where's her ring?" Crystal demanded.

His mind went blank.

Luckily, Taylor's didn't. She tightened her arms around his neck as if she'd been doing it for years. "He just asked me this morning, and the ring didn't fit. We're getting it resized."

"Likely story," Crystal jeered. "If you're really engaged, how'd he propose?"

Admiring Taylor's swift thinking, Logan fielded this one. "That's private," he said, and gazed at Taylor with what he hoped was a besotted expression.

She grinned back, merriment dancing in her eyes. Darn the woman—she was enjoying his discomfort.

"She doesn't even know you," Crystal protested. "Not like I do."

"Not possible," Logan said. "I've known her all my life."

Turning to Taylor with a challenging expression, Crystal said, "If you know so much about him, then what's his favorite color?"

"Blue," Taylor said promptly.

"Wrong," Crystal said in triumph.

"Oh, but you probably think it's green since he always wears that when he's competing. He thinks it's his lucky color."

"She's right. On both counts," Logan said, trying not to show his surprise. How'd she know that?

Crystal's face fell. She rallied quickly. "What's his dog's name?"

"Mulligan," Taylor said with a smile. "He named him that because a mulligan in golf is a do-over, so he figured the name was appropriate for his rescue dog's new life. Did *you* know *that?*"

Right again. Looked like all Logan had to do was keep his mouth shut and Taylor would do all his work for him.

Looking annoyed, Crystal continued, "And I suppose the dog likes you?"

"Of course he does," Logan interjected before Taylor could tell the truth—that Mulligan was still wary of Taylor, as he was most women. Logan figured the poor dog must have been mistreated by a woman before Logan adopted him.

"Ha, I'll believe it when I see it." Turning back to challenge Taylor, Crystal asked, "So what's his—"

"That's enough," Logan said. "I don't want you badgering my fiancée. It's time for you to leave."

Luckily, the cavalry was coming. The bartender had rounded the bar, heading toward the altercation that had everyone in the bar and restaurant craning their necks in Logan's direction.

"You can't kick me out of here," Crystal said, thrusting her chin out.

"But I can," the big man said. "You're disturbing the customers. I must insist you either sit down—at another table—and order, or leave." He glared at the reporter. "You too."

The reporter, about half his size, held up his hands as if to say he wasn't planning to cause any trouble. "You got it, bud," he said, then left, no doubt to file the juicy story.

Crystal stewed for a moment, then spat, "I know you're lying, and I'm going to stay in town until I prove it." With a final glare at Taylor, she stomped out.

Taylor pulled away and he felt a small twinge of regret. "Thanks, Adam," she said.

The beefy bartender nodded, then glanced questioningly at Logan and Ryan. "Oh," Taylor said brightly. "I don't think you've met my brother, Ryan. Ryan, this is Adam Diaz, my knight in shining armor."

She said it teasingly, but Logan gave him a sharp glance, wondering if he'd just claimed another man's girl as his own.

She continued, "And this is Logan Kelly, my...fiancé. My real knight in shining armor."

Guess not. And the ironic look she gave him was private, just between the two of them.

Adam's visage softened and he shook both men's hands. "Nice to meet you," he said. "It's good to know someone else is looking out for Taylor."

"I don't need looking after," Taylor said indignantly. "I can take care of myself."

Oh, she definitely could, but there was just something about her that brought out the protective instinct in Logan.

Adam shrugged, and the two men exchanged a knowing look. "I didn't know you were engaged," Adam said.

"It just happened this morning," Taylor said breezily. "I didn't want to say anything until I was sure Logan wanted to announce it. As you can see, he's constantly hounded by the press."

Adam's eyebrows raised as he glanced at Logan. "Oh, *that* Logan Kelly." *Whatever that meant.* "Well, I'd better get back to work. You need some time to yourselves?"

Taylor glanced doubtfully at Logan. "Uh...yeah. They need to eat their dinner before it turns cold, and probably want some privacy. Mind if we use the special events room?"

"Not at all," Adam said. "The dinner rush is over, and

your relief is due in twenty minutes. I can handle things until then."

"Thanks," Taylor said, and picked up their plates. "Guys, grab your drinks and silverware, and follow me."

"Might as well," Ryan said. "At least we'll have some privacy."

Logan followed Taylor, bemused. She was so good at managing things, he was surprised she wasn't running the whole place.

They entered an empty room, hidden from view of the other patrons, and Logan wished he could relax now, but he knew the reckoning was coming.

Sure enough, Taylor said, "You're gonna tell me what that was all about, but first, eat. I'll be back as soon as I finish my shift and clock out. I'm not leaving Adam in the lurch."

Ryan grinned at him as Taylor left. "Might as well do as she says. She always gets her way, you know."

Did she?

"I heard that," Taylor called from around the corner.

Logan grinned. Oh, well, he was still hungry and jonesing for the sub, so he bit into it. It didn't taste as good as he remembered. Maybe it was the fact that it wasn't as piping hot as when it had left the kitchen...or maybe it was because he was going to have to face Taylor and explain himself. He swallowed. "Think she's gonna kill me?" he asked Ryan.

"Oh, at the very least," Ryan said. "This'll be fun."

"Hey," Logan protested. "It was your idea to begin with. You said the only way to get rid of Crystal was to get engaged."

"Nope, you can't blame me for this one. I never said you should pretend to be engaged...much less to my *sister*."

True—he'd done that all on his own. They ate the rest

of their meal in silence as they waited for the axe to fall, Logan speculating uneasily on exactly what Taylor had meant when she said it was gonna cost him.

All too soon, Taylor rejoined them, looking tired as she grabbed a chair between them. "Okay, I get that you're trying to get rid of the bimbo by pretending to be engaged. Can't blame you there. But why pick on me?"

"Because you were available?" Logan said, then immediately regretted his impulsive reaction when he saw Taylor's face harden. "Uh, *are* you available? You dating anyone?"

"Not at the moment," Taylor said.

Thank heavens. "I'm sorry, I said that wrong. Look, Crystal has been hounding me for weeks, and your *brother* said the only thing that would stop her was my being married or engaged. So, when she said I wasn't, I jumped on the first opportunity to prove her wrong. And since you've always been such a good sport, I hoped you wouldn't mind."

Her expression didn't change much, so he guessed that explanation wasn't good enough either. She turned to glare at her brother. "And you?"

Ryan held up his hands in defense. "I thought it would send Crystal packing, so I embellished a little when Logan popped off with that zinger. I mean, it should have been perfect. She should have accepted it and moved on."

"But she didn't," Taylor said.

"No," Logan admitted. "She didn't." And now he was stuck continuing the charade. Luckily, it was with Taylor who he could trust.

"And now you're left with either having to admit to the lie, or prove you're really engaged."

"Yeah." Logan brightened. "But you told Adam we're engaged. So...?" he said hopefully.

"Because I already figured out you'd gone too far," Taylor said with a raised eyebrow.

"So...you'll go along with it?"

"Sure," Taylor said, but Logan's relief was short-lived. "But here's what you two are going to do for me...."

"Me?" Ryan protested. "Why me?"

"Because you're as much at fault as he is." Taylor narrowed her eyes at him. "Do you deny it?"

Ryan looked chastened. "I guess not."

"Okay, here's the deal," Taylor said, with the air of someone laying all her cards on the table. "You want me to pretend we're engaged, and I want you to help me start my own business."

Relieved, Logan said, "Is that all? I have plenty of money—"

"No, I don't want an investor. I have an offer of a commission waiting that will help me establish my business, but I need the time to do it properly. I can't do that while I'm working here and taking care of Dad."

"What's wrong with your father?" Logan asked. He didn't remember seeing anything amiss.

"Nothing's wrong with him, except that Mom always took care of everything. Now that she's passed, he relies on me to do everything she did—the housework, shopping, cooking, home and auto repairs, taking care of bills, reminding him to take his heart medicine.... It's like a full-time job by itself."

"He can't do that on his own?" Logan asked in disbelief. It'd been two years, after all.

"Apparently not," Taylor said. Then, ruefully, "And I haven't wanted to push him to do things on his own, not while he's still grieving." She glared at Ryan. "And my brothers haven't been any help."

Ryan looked stricken. "I didn't know."

"You didn't ask," Taylor shot back. "So *you*, Ryan, are going to take my place in helping Dad, and Logan is going to hire me to be his fiancée, so I can quit waiting tables long enough to establish myself in my hand-lettering business."

"Hand-lettering?" Logan asked. "Like calligraphy?" That didn't sound very lucrative.

"Somewhat. I do both. Copperplate calligraphy is very structured and is used for things like wedding invitations, while hand-lettering can be more creative. I draw each letter to make a piece of art. Like that." She pointed to an ornate sign painted on the mirror, announcing this area as the Barcelona Room. Far from being a standard font, it had beautiful flourishes and embellishments.

"You did that?" Logan asked in surprise. He assumed it had been done by a graphics company.

Taylor nodded.

"You've been fiddling with that stuff since you were a kid," Ryan said. "You can make a living from it?"

"I'm sure gonna try. Lana Henderson has been asking me to do wedding stationery for her, and now I have the opportunity to prove myself. All I need is the time." She glanced between the two of them. "And you two are going to give it to me."

"How much do you want to, er, hire you?" Logan asked, impressed with her passion.

"Just what I'm making now as a waitress, so I can quit and work full-time on my business. It's only until I establish myself."

That was extremely reasonable. Logan nodded.

"But hopefully he'll only need you as his fiancée for a short time, until Crystal leaves," Ryan said.

"No," Logan said. "What she's asking is fair, considering we railroaded her into this. How much time do you need?"

"I'm not sure. Three months?"

That sounded overoptimistic—didn't small businesses take longer to get established?

"Wait a minute," Ryan said. "Will you still be able to act as his fiancée and work on your business at the same time?"

"Sure, if you're helping Dad, I should have tons of time. You don't have any plans for the next three months, do you?"

Ryan grimaced, so Logan told him, "Stop 'helping.' We got her into this. We owe her. And I pay my debts."

Ryan sighed. "Yeah, I guess you're right."

Taylor held out her hand. "We have a deal?"

Logan nodded solemnly as he shook her hand. "We have a deal."

"Ryan?" Taylor asked challengingly.

"Yeah, okay," Ryan said and shook her hand.

"Okay, now details," Taylor said. "First off, we'll need a ring. I can use Mom's."

"No," Ryan said. "The stone is too small, which was all Dad could afford at the time. He always wanted to get Mom a bigger one, but she refused. Crystal will never believe Logan would be chintzy."

"No problem," Logan said, glad he could solve one problem. "We'll get one tomorrow." When Taylor looked as though she was going to protest, he added, "It's the least I can do. Besides, if you don't want to keep it," and he knew she had too much pride to do so, "then I can always sell it or something."

"He does have the cash," Ryan assured her. "It's not like it'll hurt him."

"Okay, then, what about your proposal? How did you do it?" she asked Logan.

"Uh..." Logan was stymied.

"No problem," Taylor said with a wave of her hand. "I'll come up with something suitably embarrassing and tell you how you proposed."

He supposed he deserved that.

"Do we tell our parents the truth?" she asked.

Stymied again. Wow, he really hadn't thought this through, had he?

"No," Ryan decided. "We can't trust Dad to keep it a secret. How about your mom?"

Logan shook his head. She wouldn't approve of the deception at all. "No, we'd better not tell her the truth either."

"So, it's just the three of us who know," Taylor said. "Good. It'll be easier to keep things straight then. We'll just have to avoid Match when we're together."

Yeah, the town's matchmaking dog would show up their deception in a heartbeat. "That shouldn't be hard, but there is another problem."

"Oh, yeah," Ryan said. "Mulligan."

"Yep. Crystal knows I wouldn't marry a woman unless Mulligan likes her."

"Then I'll just have to make sure Mulligan loves me," Taylor said confidently.

Good luck with that.

CHAPTER FOUR

Taylor thought she'd been doing great up until now, but her bravado faltered as the restaurant owner swept into the room. "Taylor," Beth Pietro exclaimed as she gave her a hug. "I just heard the news." She glanced at Logan. "Congratulations! I don't have to tell you that you have quite the prize in Taylor."

Logan was just a tad slow on the uptake, so Ryan nudged him with his elbow. Smiling sheepishly, Logan said, "Yes, ma'am. I know."

Before Beth could demand the details Taylor hadn't figured out yet, Taylor said, "We, uh, want to spend a lot of time together, so I'm afraid I'm going to have to give my two weeks' notice."

Beth seemed a little taken aback, but smiled ruefully. "I should have known I wouldn't be able to keep my best waitress for much longer. But we just hired someone new yesterday, so tell you what, you don't need to work those two weeks unless you want to. Consider it my engagement gift to you."

Stunned, Taylor gaped at her. Not have to deal with

drunks anymore or greasy, stained clothes? *Count me in.* "That's incredibly generous. Thank you."

Beth hugged her again. "Just make sure you invite me to the wedding."

"Of course." Easy to promise when there wasn't going to be one.

Beth breezed out, and Taylor glanced at Logan and Ryan. "That was easier than I expected."

Ryan nodded. "Yeah, but gossip moves swiftly in this town. You'd better tell Dad and Logan's mom before they find out from someone else."

"Good point," Logan said. "Shall we go?"

The guys paid their tab, and they all left, Logan riding with Taylor so they could strategize. He filled up a huge amount of space in her little Mini Cooper and was entirely too close...just what she'd been trying to avoid since he'd come home. How was she supposed to keep her feelings hidden when he was *right there?* It was hard enough to do when he was living in the house, even harder when she was alone with him in the car...but pretending to be engaged? *What was I thinking?*

Obviously, she'd thought he looked desperate for rescue. How could she refuse to help him, especially when the woman pursuing him was obviously all wrong for him? He needed someone to love him for himself. *Someone like me....*

Logan interrupted her thoughts. "How did you know all that?"

"All what?"

"About my favorite color, Mulligan's name..."

She rolled her eyes. "I've known you all my life, remember? And I'm very observant." Too observant when it came to him, but she couldn't let him know that. "You've mentioned those things a time or two. Or Ryan has."

"Oh," he said, accepting her explanation at face value. "Sorry, I don't know as much about you...."

"No biggie. We'll figure it out. Besides, you probably know more than you think. But first, how are we going to tell Dad?"

Logan took in a deep breath. "Well, he's an old-fashioned guy. I'll need to ask for his permission."

Such a guy thing. But Dad would love it. "Okay, good. If he asks, tell him what Ryan said. We've been carrying on a romance secretly for years when you were home, and you've been wanting to ask me to marry you, but I refused until you retired and settled down in Dogwood. When I finally agreed, you figured you'd better ask for the old man's permission first." She glanced ruefully at him. "Though we both know he'd never say no to you."

He glanced at her. "You're really good at this."

"Lying? Gee, thanks." Almost as good as him admitting he chose her as his fake fiancée because she was the only one available and a "good sport."

"No, I didn't mean that. I meant you're really fast on your feet, and your imagination allows you to spin stories out of thin air like it's nothing."

She shrugged. It was easy when she'd daydreamed all her life about Logan falling for her.

"So, Mom will probably want to know—how did I propose?" He looked at her warily, and she grinned.

"Don't worry—I won't really embarrass you. I just said that to...you know."

"Get revenge?"

She laughed. "Sort of. Look, what's logical? We don't have the ring yet, and we can't fool our parents into thinking we do. So...let's see. You saw me this morning and were so overcome by my beauty and chocolate chip pancakes that you had to propose right then and there at the breakfast table." Yeah, right. She paused for a moment. "After Dad left for work and Ryan went up to his room, that is."

"Not very romantic," Logan protested.

Taylor's eyebrows raised. He wanted romance? Who knew? "So how would you have done it? Remember, we told Crystal we were engaged this morning."

"Uh...I don't know. It would certainly be more thought-out than that." He thought for a moment. "Breakfast was the first time we were alone since I got back to Dogwood, and I was afraid I'd lose you to someone like Adam if I didn't pop the question, so I dropped to one knee and gave an impassioned speech I'd been rehearsing for weeks about how I couldn't live without you." He glanced at her in question.

"That works." Though she'd sure like to hear that speech for herself.

"But we'll tell the parents I'm such a thoughtful guy that I didn't get a ring, figuring you'd like to pick out your own. We told a little fib to Crystal to get her off our back, but we're going to Colorado Springs tomorrow to find the perfect one."

"Why Colorado Springs? We have a jewelry store here, you know."

"I know, but this way we're less likely to run into Crystal or someone we know who could prove we weren't telling the truth."

"That definitely works. See, you're good at lying, too."

He winced. "I'm sorry. I know this is a huge imposition. You sure you're okay with it?"

"Absolutely. I'm getting what I want as well, remember?" She thought about patting his knee in reassurance, but decided it was better not to touch him. Then again, she'd have to, if she was his fiancée, right? "But if we've been hiding a secret romance for so long, we need to be...less awkward with each other." When he gave her a questioning look, she added, "You know, hugging and stuff."

"Hugging and stuff?" he repeated, obviously amused.

Feeling her face heat, Taylor said, "You know what I mean. We'll probably need to hold hands at least and look lovingly into each other's eyes. You know—all that mushy stuff newly engaged couples do."

"I can do that," Logan said. "It's like acting a part. I've had to do that often enough on the tour." He grimaced, and Taylor wondered about the story behind that. "How about you?"

She would have to "pretend" to the world that she loved Logan Kelly, while pretending to Logan that she didn't. "Sure, piece of cake," she lied.

She pulled up into their driveway and watched as Logan carefully unfolded himself from her tiny car. "No time like the present," Logan said, and held out his hand.

She took it reluctantly, and Logan curled his fingers between hers. "Let's do this," he said. "Let's go get mushy."

Her heart beat double-time and heat suffused her body as she clutched Logan's hand tighter. Hopefully, he thought she was just getting a head start on the playacting.

They entered the house hand in hand, and Dad looked up from where he was reading the paper in his recliner, obviously surprised. Mulligan jumped up from his dog bed in the corner and ran to greet Logan. "Coach," Logan said as he bent to pet the dog, "could I speak to you for a moment? Privately?"

Taking that as her cue to get lost, Taylor motioned to Ryan, who'd arrived just behind them. "Come upstairs with me. I have something to show you."

They entered her small studio and Taylor dragged him to her computer. "Now, here's the schedule."

"Schedule?" Ryan repeated in astonishment.

"This is the timeline I use for taking care of the house and Dad. I've got it all spelled out—all you need to do is follow it. Plus help Dad out with anything else he needs." At his shocked look, she narrowed her eyes at him. "You're not going back on your word, are you?"

He scanned the printed list, his eyes widening in dismay. "No, I just— I had no idea you did so much."

Taylor hid a smile. It would be good for him to find out. "Now you do."

"And schedules and everything? You're so...efficient. I always thought of you as the artsy type."

"Like artsy types can't be competent?" When he gestured helplessly, she added, "I've had to be, in order to make everything work. Now, look at the schedule. Tonight, you have to cook dinner for Dad and wash the dishes afterward. Tomorrow is laundry day." She paused. "You do know where the laundry room is, don't you? And actually how to do laundry?"

"Of course I do," Ryan said. "Mom taught all of us, remember?"

Yeah, though Taylor didn't remember Ryan actually ever doing any. "You sure you're up for this?"

For some reason, that seemed to challenge Ryan's manhood or something. He straightened up and said, "I can do it. If I'd realized how much you did, I would have done something about it before now."

"Like what?" Taylor asked, intrigued by how her brother's mind worked.

"Like—"

"Taylor, can you come down here?" Dad yelled from downstairs, cutting Ryan off.

Time to face the music. Taylor went slowly downstairs, Ryan right behind her, as her father held out his arms. "I couldn't be happier, sweetie. Logan is the best man in the world."

As she went into her father's arms, she gazed helplessly over his shoulder at Logan. She hadn't known how guilty this would make her feel. "I know, Dad. Me too."

"Naw," Ryan said, "he's the groom. *I'm* the best man."

Ryan's joking helped make the moment a little less awkward.

"So," her father said. "What's for dinner?"

"I don't know—ask Ryan," Taylor said gleefully. "He'll get dinner for you while we go tell Logan's mom."

"Uh, we already ate," Ryan said as Logan put a leash on Mulligan and opened the door. "How do you feel about take-out, Dad?"

Logan chuckled as he led her to his car, one that had a lot more leg room than Taylor's Mini. "You've got him started helping already, have you?"

"You betcha," Taylor said brightly. It sure felt good to have some of the burden off her shoulders, though she suspected it wouldn't be long before Ryan was calling for help.

Then, as she buckled herself into the roomy vehicle, Logan set Mulligan in her lap and said, "Be good."

Was he talking to the dog or to her? Either way, they regarded each other warily. Mulligan didn't growl at her like Logan said he did to other women, but his stiffened body showed he wasn't exactly thrilled with her presence either. She gingerly ran her fingers through his soft fur and crooned, "That's a good boy."

He wouldn't relax, but he didn't snap or growl at her either. Taylor considered that a win. Hopefully, Logan's mother would be a little more accepting. "How do you think your mom will react?" she asked, suddenly nervous.

"Oh, fine," he said as they drove toward her house. "I think she'll just be glad I'm settling down, as she calls it. She's always wanted grandchildren."

Taylor swallowed hard. "Grandchildren? Isn't that getting a bit ahead of ourselves?"

"That's where Mom's mind will go, I promise you." He grinned at her. "Don't worry—I don't expect you to go that far."

"Glad to hear it," she said in a small voice. The thought of what it would take to accomplish that had her squirming in her seat. *Don't even think about it,* she told herself. *Not gonna happen.* Darn it.

Luckily, he was right. His mother, Sherry, said she was thrilled to have another woman in the family, and declared that she'd known all along they were perfect together. Taylor smiled back, not knowing what to say to that.

"So, have you set a date yet?" Sherry asked. "Are you thinking about a June wedding? It'll be kind of tight, unless you want a very small affair. Or are you thinking next June?"

Whoa—that had snowballed rather quickly. She glanced at Logan in indecision. They hadn't talked about that.

Logan held up his hands defensively. "We haven't discussed that yet. Let us enjoy this time together first, okay? I've been gone a long time."

"Okay," Sherry said and regarded Taylor with an expression that was both hopeful and sympathetic at the same time. "But I'd love to help you with the wedding, if you want. I know you must be missing your mom at this time."

Despite herself, Taylor felt tears welling in her eyes.

Everyone was just too darned nice about this fake engagement. "Thanks," Taylor said thickly. "I'd love that." What else could she say?

As Sherry hugged her, Taylor gazed helplessly at Logan who looked equally at a loss. They'd really committed themselves now.

But when this was finally over, how could they possibly tell the people they loved that they were lying?

CHAPTER FIVE

LOGAN SPENT A SLEEPLESS NIGHT, having second, third, and even fourth thoughts about the scheme the three of them had concocted. How could he convince everyone he was in love with Taylor, when he knew so little about her? Most of his life, he'd thought of her as Ryan's pesky little sister. It was hard to go from that to thinking of her as the woman he was going to marry—pretend, of course.

There was much to admire about Taylor—the way she took care of her father and brothers, her work ethic, her organizational ability, and her ability to think fast on her feet. But that wasn't enough reason to convince people he was in love with her.

Then again, there had been that spark between them just before he left the first time for the tour. They'd been alone as his and Ryan's farewell barbecue wound down, sitting together in the Nashes' small gazebo. She'd seemed so fresh, innocent, and full of dreams. And who could resist that hero worship in her eyes?

Not Logan. Not then. He'd leaned in just a little as she

raised her face eagerly to his...and then Ryan had called his name. Good thing, or he might have done something he regretted. He'd avoided being alone with her ever since, but, given her reactions today, it seemed she really had outgrown her crush on him. Though a bit sad that he'd fallen off her pedestal, he realized he could use the memory of that spark to ignite some of the feelings he needed to show in order to pull this off. It wouldn't be difficult. At all.

Starting now. She came down the stairs in jeans and a pink fuzzy sweater. Though he'd always gone for sophisticated, long-haired brunettes of a more...voluptuous nature, small, intense blondes with a pixie look were definitely in the running. It wouldn't be hard to recapture that spark. It might even be fun.

She glanced at him. "Something wrong?"

He grinned. "No, no. Just thinking about what we need to do."

"Okay, then, let's do it. Ryan said he'll stave off reporters and groupies while we head to Colorado Springs. If we leave now, we should get there just as the jewelry store opens."

"Sounds good," Logan said, and escorted her to his car. Luckily, no one was lurking out there this early, so they were able to get away without incident.

Taylor was pretty focused on her smartphone from the moment she got in the car. Good thing no one was watching, or they'd wonder why his fiancée was ignoring him. He kind of wondered that himself. Hard to spark a fire when there was no tinder.

"I thought I'd stop and grab us some us something to eat and some coffee," he said, pulling up to the Crack-of-Dawn Donut Shop order window. "How do you like your coffee?"

"I don't drink coffee," Taylor said absently as she continued texting. "But chai sounds good."

He smiled ruefully. "I guess I should know that about my fiancée. What about doughnuts?"

"I prefer muffins," she said with a smile. "I'll have one of their banana nut ones."

He placed their order at the first window, telling them what Taylor wanted and ordering a bear claw and black coffee for himself. As he headed toward the pick-up window, he said, "Do you really think we can pull this off? I mean, I didn't even know you don't drink coffee." He glanced at her ruefully. "I'm not as observant as you are."

Taylor paused in her texting to look up at him with a grin. "That's okay. You're a guy. No one expects you to be."

"*I* do." He prided himself on knowing the women he dated very well and catering to their whims. Did Taylor even have whims?

"Okay, then observe. You just learned something now, didn't you?"

"I guess," he said as he paid for their breakfast and headed toward Highway 50 and Colorado Springs. "But what if someone asks something about you and I don't know the answer?"

"You could always make something up," Taylor said, continuing to text. "But you have a point. You know how, in all those romantic comedies, someone asks a question and both people fumble totally different answers, making it obvious they're both lying?"

"Yeah, that's what I'm afraid of—giving away the deception."

She slanted a glance at him. "Let's not do that."

"Okay," Logan said with relief. "And since you're much faster on the uptake, I'll let you do the answering for both of us."

"Works for me," Taylor said. "And if you make something up when I'm not around, let me know so I don't contradict you."

"I can do that."

Her phone rang then and she answered it. "No," she said curtly. He glanced at her in surprise, and she rolled her eyes. "No, I'm not interested in an interview now or ever. Don't call me again." She stabbed the hang-up button, looking frustrated. "Stupid reporters," she muttered. "I'm turning off the ringer." She did that, then typed furiously on her phone again.

Feeling unaccountably irked, Logan asked, "What's so fascinating on your phone?"

"I'm trying to get ahead of the rumors," she said distractedly. "Letting my friends know of our engagement and why I didn't tell them I was seeing you before. I'm doing group texts to save time."

"Oh." He hadn't thought about how it would affect her relationships. "What excuse did you come up with?"

"You're coming across great," she assured him. "You wanted to keep our relationship a secret for my sake, to help me avoid rabid reporters and deranged groupies. They think it's very sweet of you."

"Yay, me," Logan said, raising his coffee in salute to himself.

"And now we're sneaking off so we can have some alone time." She raised the phone in his direction. "Smile for the camera."

He gave her an "are you kidding me?" look, but she took the picture anyway.

"Perfect," she declared. "Now I can tell them I need to get off the phone to pay more attention to you."

He had to admit that's exactly what he would have requested, had she really been his fiancée.

She sighed and rested her phone in her lap. "Boy, that was harder than I thought. They're all excited for me, but there's a lot of hinting going on about bridesmaid choices and wedding plans."

"I'm sorry. I know this is a great inconvenience for you. Are you sure you really want to continue the...engagement?" Did she even like him anymore? He thought she did, but it didn't seem that way.

"It's kind of late to think about that now, isn't it?"

"Not really. We could always have an argument and break it off." He hurried to say, "You'd dump me, of course. I can be a real jerk sometimes."

"Nope, sorry. You're not getting out of it now, especially since I already quit my job. I sent you an email last night with my pay records so you'll know what this will cost you."

Efficient of her, though he hadn't checked his email yet this morning.

"And I accepted Lana Henderson's offer for the first real commission in my new business." She paused then glanced at him. "You're not having second thoughts, are you?"

"No, of course not," he lied. He couldn't do that to her, now that she'd totally uprooted her life to accommodate him.

Her phone buzzed and she glanced at it. "Lana is sending the list of addresses over now. I can get started this afternoon."

She was usually very focused and determined, so he'd never seen her look this happy and relaxed. She'd always been attractive, but her smile made her stunning.

"This afternoon?" Logan repeated. "Shouldn't we be spending more time together? As an engaged couple, I mean."

"Sure, but that doesn't mean we need to be joined at the hip. Don't you have anything else to do?"

"Not really. I thought I'd go out to the driving range sometime soon, then find a physical therapist for my shoulder."

"Okay, good. Dad's working at the pro shop today. If you give him some notice, he'd love to show you off to his buddies. As for the physical therapist, do you have someone in mind?"

"No, not really. Do you know of a good one in Dogwood?"

"When Dad injured his knee, he really liked Margaret Hansell of Heart and Mind Healing Therapy."

"If she's good enough for Coach, she's good enough for me."

"Okay, let me see if she has an appointment available." She typed furiously on her phone, then said, "She has an appointment available at 10:00 tomorrow morning where she can do an evaluation of your shoulder and determine what you need. Sound good?"

Bemused, Logan nodded.

"Okay, I'll book it for you and text you the info."

Sure enough, his phone dinged. "Thanks. No wonder Coach relies on you so much." It was like having his own private secretary, though he would never say that to her.

"Yeah, I guess I'm too efficient sometimes," Taylor said with a sigh.

"And your father takes advantage of that?"

"Yeah, but it's partially my fault, too. I let him."

"Not any longer. Now it's Ryan's turn to be taken advantage of," Logan said with a smile.

"If he's up to the job."

"Oh, he is," Logan assured her. "Who do you think did

most of the bookings and travel arrangements on the tour for me?"

"Huh. Never thought about it. Ryan does that?"

"Yep. He doesn't just carry around golf clubs, you know. A good caddy is much more than that. He scouts the course and suggests which club to use, takes care of my equipment, keeps my yardage books, helps me keep my head on straight."

"Plus runs interference with reporters and groupies?" she said with a lift of her eyebrow.

"That, too. Ryan actually does more than most caddies. He's almost like my agent."

"Hmm. Guess I don't give him enough credit. As a matter of fact, after I gave him Dad's schedule, I expected him to have panicked by now and texted me at least twice." She glanced down at the phone. "Nothing so far."

"Disappointed you're not indispensable?" he asked teasingly.

"Are you kidding? I love it."

He laughed. "Well, we have to figure out why I think you're indispensable to me."

"I've cleared the decks for now and turned my cell phone to vibrate, so let's get to know each other better."

"Sure. What would you like to know?"

"Well, I'm curious. Ryan doesn't talk about the tour life much, but the media makes it sound so glamorous. Is it?"

Logan sighed. "Depends on what you mean by glamorous. Sure, there's good money in it if you're in the top 125, but that's only if you make the cut and get to play. If you don't, you still have all the expenses of travel, hotel, food, the works—and no prize money to show for it."

"You don't have a problem making the cut, do you?"

"Not anymore, but I sure did at the beginning. Ryan and I spent a lot of time in cheap hotels back then."

"What about sponsorships, the swag, and the PGA parties I've heard so much about?"

"I have to admit it was exciting in the beginning and went to my head a bit, but it gets old pretty quickly." He sighed. "I love golf, but I don't love feeling like a commodity to be bought and sold."

"Is that why you're retiring?"

"Partially. The shoulder injury is just an excuse. But don't tell anyone else that," he added quickly. When she mimed zipping her lips and throwing away the key, he added, "I set out to prove myself on the tour, and I did that." Several times over, in fact. "But life on a PGA tour isn't conducive to a stable family life, and I watched too many relationships implode because of it. Now I want to move on to a different phase of life. Settle down somewhere permanently."

"Figure out what you want to be when you grow up?" Taylor suggested.

"Something like that."

Taylor nodded sagely. "So that's why you came back to Dogwood? Let Match help you find your soul mate?"

"Something like that. But I don't want to let Crystal and her ilk think I'm up for grabs now that I'm retired. She is definitely *not* what I'm looking for."

"If Crystal isn't your type, what *are* you looking for?" she asked curiously.

"Something stable. Someone real. Someone I can make a life with. You know, the whole picket fence, kids, and a dog sort of life." He didn't know why he felt so comfortable confiding in Taylor. Maybe pulling off this deception would be easier than he thought.

"Uh huh," she said, though there was doubt in her tone.

"You don't think I can do that?"

"Oh, I think you can find that...eventually. But it'll be

difficult to find the woman of your dreams while you're pretend-engaged to me."

"Yeah, there is that." He thought for a moment. "Not a problem. Once we get rid of Crystal, we can both get on with our own lives." He cast her a glance. "Do you want the same thing? Picket fence, etc.?"

"Yeah, someday. When I meet the right guy."

For the rest of the drive to the Springs, they shared their likes and dislikes with each other. They both liked action movies, but their tastes diverged in other areas. He liked horror and she preferred romantic comedies. For food, they both ate pretty much anything, though Taylor was a little more picky about where she ate, having worked as a waitress for so long.

When they reached the jewelry store, he parked then said, "I asked Ryan to call ahead so we can get a private showing." When she looked alarmed, he added, "Just in case there are any golf fans shopping there today. To avoid any gossip."

She nodded. "Good idea."

"But we still need to act like a real engaged couple. Ready to get mushy again?"

She laughed, just as he hoped. "I'm ready."

They got out of the car and he linked her fingers with his. It still felt a little awkward, but not uncomfortable. In fact, it was rather nice, if she'd just loosen up a little.

He ushered her in and introduced himself.

"Oh, Mr. Kelly," the salesman said, smiling. "We have a room ready for you. If you'll follow me? Our manager will be happy to help you."

The manager, a sleek brunette, introduced herself as Alexandra and, as they seated themselves, she said, "I understand you're here for an engagement ring?"

Logan nodded, and looked lovingly into Taylor's eyes.

"That's right. She said yes, making me the happiest man on earth."

Taylor blushed, adding credence to the lie. But only the two of them knew it was embarrassment instead of pleasure.

"Congratulations," Alexandra said. "I didn't know your budget or your preferences, but I took the liberty of pulling some possible rings for you that span a range of prices."

He glanced down at the tray of rings she presented, and noticed that the stones were rather large on all of them. He didn't know anything about jewelry, but he suspected that range she mentioned probably started at the high end. No problem—he could afford it. "What do you like?" he asked Taylor.

Her eyes widened as she took in the flashing row of diamonds. "Uh, what about this one?" she asked, pointing to the smallest one. "How much is it?"

When Alexandra told them the price—around five thousand dollars—Taylor blanched.

It wouldn't exactly make him look chintzy, but Crystal knew he could afford more than that, and would be even more suspicious.

"No, sweetie," he said gently. "Don't worry about the money. I can afford the best, and that's what you deserve. You know your family would like you to have the best, don't you? How about this one?" He pointed to one that looked both classy and expensive, to his eye anyway. "How much is that one?"

When Alexandra quoted a price about double the other ring, Taylor gasped and backed away from the table. "No, no, no. I can't do this."

Whoa. What on earth had happened to his unflappable Taylor?

CHAPTER SIX

TEN THOUSAND DOLLARS? Taylor couldn't think, couldn't breathe. That was a heck of a lot of money for a pretend engagement. She glanced at Logan in panic.

He wasn't angry with her, thank goodness. Instead, he turned to Alexandra and said, "Can you give us a few minutes?"

"Of course," the sleek woman said and gathered up the tray full of expensive rings, leaving them alone in the small room.

"What's wrong?" he asked, looking concerned.

"I-I'm not sure. When I heard those prices, I just panicked." He must think she was a total idiot.

"Why?" he asked gently. "You knew we were coming for an engagement ring."

She didn't really understand it herself. But...no one had ever spent anywhere near that amount on her, and it just felt wrong.

Don't you think you're worth it? a small voice asked inside her.

Uh...maybe? But not like this, not when he was going to

have to spend so much for a ring he might not be able to resell. "It's so expensive, and I work a lot with my hands. What if I knock the stone out or something? What if I lose it?"

He put an arm around her. "If that's all that's bothering you, we'll get it insured," Logan assured her.

Wow, that hug sure felt good. She couldn't help herself —she leaned into it. "I-I don't know. You shouldn't have to spend that much money on me. I mean, on a pretend engagement."

"We do if we want it to look real. They all know I make a lot of money, and I wouldn't have chosen an inexpensive ring to give my fiancée."

No, she couldn't let him spend that kind of money. It would be wrong. But she just shook her head. "Can't we just get a cubic zirconia or something? No one could tell the difference."

"Would you feel better about it if we did?"

She nodded vigorously.

"Okay," Logan said. "How about I ask Alexandra to show us some cubic zirconias and other stones?"

Relief filled her. "That would be great. Tell her I'm concerned about blood diamonds that fund wars." It wasn't really a lie.

"Okay, what style do you think you'd like?"

"I'm not sure. Nothing too fussy—that's just not me— but something simple, elegant, and...creative?"

"Okay, let me talk to Alexandra and see what she can do." He grinned at her. "But this time, don't ask about the prices. Just get something you like, and let me worry about the money, okay?"

She gave him a wobbly smile. "Okay. But what will Alexandra think of me?"

"Don't worry about it—I'm sure she sees bridal jitters

all the time." He stood up, taking his wonderful warmth with him. "I'll explain that's all it is, and ask her to bring some rings that are more to your liking, okay?"

"Sounds good," Taylor said. As soon as he left the room, she berated herself for acting like such a moron. How could she pull this off if she reacted so strongly to a simple ring?

Simple? Ha. Nothing simple about those rings.

Logan returned then, saying, "Alexandra understands perfectly, and is pulling some more rings for you to look at." He took her hand, looking at her reassuringly. "No matter what ring you choose, it'll be okay. Just don't make me look chintzy, all right?"

She laughed. "Okay, you got it." He was being so nice about her momentary panic attack, she liked him even more.

He kept her hand clasped in his. Taylor was sure it was for show, but whatever his reason, it did help keep her calm as Alexandra returned with another tray of rings.

"I'm sorry—" Taylor began, but Alexandra stopped her.

"No need to apologize. It happens more often than you think. And more and more people are forgoing diamonds in favor of engagement rings that more fit their style. Now, do any of these catch your eye?"

Relieved that Alexandra was making it so easy, Taylor glanced down at the glittering rings. There were a few diamond-looking stones that must be fake cubic zirconias, though she couldn't tell the difference, along with colored stones in a variety of settings—emeralds, sapphires, rubies, and others she didn't recognize right off.

One caught her eye right away—one with a pink round stone, tiny diamonds intermittently spaced around it to make them look like petals. "It looks like a flower," she said with pleasure.

"You have a good eye," Alexandra said. "This round-cut stone is morganite, which is becoming increasingly popular for engagement rings, especially among those concerned about conflict diamonds. It's in the beryl family, like emeralds and aquamarines. And the small diamonds around it are certified conflict-free. Would you like to try it on?"

"Sure," Taylor said. Logan slid it on her finger, acting the part of the perfect fiancé, and the ring fit perfectly. She loved the way it sparkled on her finger. It was a happy-looking ring, not at all stuffy or pretentious.

"I like it," Logan declared. "Is that the one?"

She'd never owned anything so pretty. "I-I think so." She started to ask the price, then remembered she'd promised not to. When the other two looked at her expectantly, she told herself to stop being an idiot and show her appreciation. "Yes, it is," she said in a more definite tone and grinned. "I love it."

That seemed to be the right thing to say, because they both beamed at her.

Alexandra rose. "If you'd like to stay here for a few minutes, your fiancé and I can finalize the purchase."

"Sure," Taylor said. If she didn't know how much it cost, she couldn't stress about it. "Don't forget the insurance," she told Logan. Well, she might still stress a little bit.

As Logan went off with the saleswoman, she checked her phone. There were some more texts from her friends—mostly silliness—and, to please them, she took a selfie with her left hand and its glittering new accessory held nonchalantly up to her face. She sent it off with a grin. There—they'd love that.

But the next text she received was from her dad.

Will you and Logan be back in town for lunch?

I think so, she texted back, admiring the way her new

ring flashed when she typed. *Did you have something in mind?*

The guys would like to meet him. Can you meet us at the 19th Hole at noon?

Let me ask him. And, as luck would have it, he walked in just then.

"Ready?" Logan asked.

"Yes. Hey, Dad wants to meet us for lunch at noon at the 19th Hole so he can show you off to his buddies. You up for that?"

"For Coach? Anything," Logan said.

"Okay, I'll let him know." She texted back, *We'll be there.*

Dad sent back a thumbs-up emoji, and she smiled up at Logan. "Thanks. He'll love this."

"No problem." Logan glanced down at her hand. "It looks good on you."

She held her hand out, admiring the stone again. "It does, doesn't it?" He laughed, and she added, "But don't worry. I'm not planning on keeping it."

"I'm not worried. It's not like you entrapped me or anything."

"True. Though Crystal might think I did." She glanced critically at the ring. "Do you think it's enough to convince her?"

"Sure. If not, tell her Tiffany's introduced the morganite stone, naming it after J.P. Morgan."

"Is that true?"

"That's what Alexandra just told me. And if it's good enough for them..."

"Okay. Good to know." All she knew was that she loved it. Too bad she wasn't going to be able to keep it...or him.

THEY MET her father and Ryan at the golf course's bar and grill right at noon, and Taylor grinned as her dad proudly introduced Logan as his future son-in-law to three of his best buds. They commandeered a table, and started talking golf immediately after they ordered lunch.

She pulled Ryan to the outskirts of the group, so the other guys could grill Logan on his golf career. She and her brother were pretty much ignored, so they held their own private conversation.

Her brother rolled his eyes. "Looks like a mere caddy and fiancée aren't important enough to warrant attention alongside the famous Logan Kelly."

She laughed. "I don't mind. And surely you're used to it."

He grinned back at her. "Yeah, and I don't mind either. You'd think it would go to his head, but it doesn't."

One of the many things she admired about him. Changing the subject, she asked, "So how's it going caring for Dad? In over your head yet?"

"Not at all," Ryan declared. "I talked with him this morning after you left and told him he'd been taking advantage of you."

"Oh, Ryan, you didn't." That wasn't what she wanted at all.

"Yes, I did. And he admitted he relied on you too much."

"He did?" she said in surprise. She'd thought he was oblivious.

"Yeah, well, I kind of pushed him to admit that he couldn't expect you to do everything for him after you're married."

"But you know we won't—" She broke off, realizing where they were and who might be listening in.

Ryan lowered his voice. "Well, you're bound to get married sooner or later...to someone."

True. She lowered her voice as well. "So he's going to do everything himself?" Yeah, right. As if that would happen.

"Well, no," Ryan admitted. "But I did tell him I'd help him hire someone to clean for him, maybe cook some meals and do his laundry, and find someone to teach him how to take care of his own money. Logan's mom can help with that. Plus, since he has no problem using his phone to text, I showed him how to use the calendar function and reminders so he can keep track of everything himself."

"And he agreed to all this?" She glanced doubtfully at the man who'd seemed so helpless just this morning.

"Yeah," Ryan said. "He can afford it. And I think he'll enjoy being independent." He frowned at her. "You're okay with this, right? I mean, he's relied on you for so long...."

"Absolutely," she exclaimed and sat back in surprise. "Wow. And here I thought you'd be scrambling to take care of him. Instead, you're helping him find resources to do it himself."

"What?" Ryan asked with a lift of his eyebrow. "You thought you were the only organized one in the family?"

Well, yeah, but she wouldn't admit that to him. "Clearly not. I just didn't think he would be willing to accept help from anyone outside the family."

"Well, he wasn't at first, but I talked him into it."

"Kudos, Ryan." She raised her water glass to him in a mock toast. "You've just made my life infinitely easier."

"Thanks, but there's something you need to know—" He broke off, staring over her shoulder and saying, "Uh oh."

She closed her eyes. "Don't tell me. Crystal, or the reporter?"

"Crystal."

Sure enough, the blonde wandered over to their table

in a tight dress that advertised she was on the hunt. "I thought I'd find you here," she cooed, ignoring everyone at the table except for Logan. She glanced around. "What are you doing in this dump?"

Dump? Taylor glanced around the restaurant, seeing it with new eyes. True, the pub-like décor hadn't changed since the place had opened, back in the eighties, and it was beginning to look a little shabby around the edges. It could do with some refurbishing, but she wouldn't call it a dump, exactly.

"This is a private conversation," her father told the woman. "And this place is not a dump."

"Could've fooled me," Crystal muttered. Then, to Logan, she said, "You know, I've been talking to people around town. No one seems to believe you and *that woman* are engaged. No one even saw you two together. I knew it —you're just playing hard to get, but trust me, it's not necessary."

Logan looked weary of the whole situation, and Taylor felt for him. Did he have to put up with this kind of thing all the time?

But help came from an unexpected source. Her father stood, looking grim. "'That woman' as you call her, is my daughter. Logan kept their dating quiet out of concern for unwanted attention." He looked Crystal up and down. "Looks like he was right to do so."

"Oh, yeah?" Crystal scoffed. "Then why aren't they sitting together?"

Taylor got up and walked around to put her left hand on Logan's shoulder. With the other, she gave him a warning squeeze, reminding him to let her talk. "Because I was being polite and letting these gentlemen talk to him. After all, he's mine for the rest of our lives." She wiggled her left hand in emphasis, letting the ring flash and speak for her as she gave Logan a loving look. He returned her gaze in kind, amusement simmering in his eyes.

Crystal glared at the ring. "I don't believe it—"

"Your belief is not required," her father said firmly.

Another man stood—Hal Warner, the septuagenarian owner of the golf club. "Nor is your presence," the small, stooped man said in a tone that brooked no argument. "I own this 'dump,' young lady, and I reserve the right to refuse service to anyone. Leave now, or I'll call security."

Her father's other cronies stood as well, creating a four-man wall that blocked Crystal's view of Logan and Taylor.

"Logan, are you going to let them treat me like this?" Crystal demanded.

When Logan kept silent except for a speaking glance at Ryan, her brother drawled, "Looks like he is. Now, why don't you let me escort you out."

It was a statement, not a question, and Ryan showed Crystal to the door. The four-man blockade finally sat when she was gone.

"I apologize for that," Logan said with a sigh. "She's totally oblivious to the fact that I don't want to have anything to do with her." He glanced at Hal. "And this place is obviously not a dump."

Hal sighed. "Well, I know it needs some updating, but times have been tough lately, and I'd rather spend what money I have on the course."

"Makes perfect sense," her father said, clapping Hal on the back. "But, with your approval, I'd like to have their engagement party here. Keep out the riff-raff like her."

"Of course," Hal said, as Taylor stood, stunned.

"Engagement party?" she said with a squeak. Her fingers tightened on Logan's arm and shoulder. *Please, no.*

Her father grinned. "Sorry to tell you this way, but Logan's mother and I can't let you get engaged without celebrating, now can we? We've got it all planned. All you need to do is show up."

Taylor dropped into the chair next to Logan and glanced accusingly at Ryan, who had just returned to the table. Was that what he wanted to tell her? She sure wished he'd let her know ahead of time so she could head this off. He shrugged apologetically.

Logan put his hand reassuringly over hers. "That's not really necessary, Coach."

"Of course it is. Isn't that right, fellows?" Her father looked around at the other men and they all echoed their approval.

Taylor swallowed hard. How could she let this happen?

Then again, how could she not? She couldn't disappoint her father and Logan's mother. That wasn't even on the table. *Be gracious,* she reminded herself. *He thinks he's doing a good thing.* "Thank you, Dad. It's very sweet of you. But we insist—absolutely no gifts."

Logan echoed her sentiments, adding, "Good idea to have it here, so we'll have to keep it small and intimate. Just friends and family."

Her father looked a bit disappointed. Sheesh—knowing him, he'd planned on inviting the whole town. Thank goodness Logan had a level head.

As Taylor gave her father a fake smile to match their equally fake engagement, she told herself it was just a party, not a life-long commitment. How bad could it be?

The lunch broke up after that, and Taylor headed home with Logan and Ryan. "Why didn't you warn me?" Taylor demanded of Ryan, twisting to glare at him in the back seat.

He shrugged. "I tried to, but there didn't seem to be an opportunity to bring it up."

"What's the problem?" Logan asked. "Pretend it's just any old party."

"You're forgetting that all the attention will be on us, that they'll expect us to be all mushy and stuff."

Logan grinned. "So? We can do that, right?"

"I'm not sure," Ryan said. "There are some very shrewd people in this town. Whenever you two get close, it's obvious you're a bit uncomfortable, Taylor." He snapped his fingers. "I know—you have to practice kissing."

Taylor gaped at him. "Ki-kissing?"

"Yes, kissing. Each other," Ryan explained as if she were a couple of tacos short of a fiesta platter. "If you can get comfortable doing that, you should have no problem pulling off a deception at the party. You know they're going to clink their glasses with silverware to make you kiss."

Since when was he so knowledgeable about engagement parties? Taylor moistened her lips and willed herself not to look at Logan. What if he looked disgusted? Or bored? Either way, she didn't think she could take it.

"I'm game," Logan said.

She risked a glance at him then, and he winked at her.

She jerked her head back to stare out the windshield. *Good grief. What do I do now?* On one hand, she'd always daydreamed about what it would have been like if Logan had actually followed through on that almost-kiss long ago. On the other hand, how would she be able to keep her feelings a secret if she did kiss him? "You really think that's a good idea?" she asked Logan.

"Yes, I do. Ryan's right. You look like a startled deer in the headlights every time I touch you."

"I've just never..."

"Never what? Been kissed?"

"Of course I've been kissed," she snapped. Though never by Logan. "I've just never been...pretend-kissed."

He chuckled. "Well, that makes two of us. But I'm willing to practice if you are."

"Yeah," Ryan chimed in. "You gotta make it look good if we're going to get rid of Crystal."

She couldn't believe she was in this situation. Kissing practice, for heaven's sake?

Go on. You know you want to, a little voice inside her said.

More than that, the guys were right. They needed to make this whole thing seem more natural, as if they were a normal happily engaged couple. Not only to keep up her end of the bargain, but a small part of her really liked the idea of needling Crystal. She sighed. "Okay, I'll do it."

Logan gave her an odd look. "Why the heavy sigh? You think it'll be that bad?"

That snapped her back to her regular snarky self. "Well, that's up to you, isn't it?"

Ryan chortled from the back as Logan raised his eyebrow and said softly, "Challenge accepted."

CHAPTER SEVEN

Whoa. *Challenge accepted?* Taylor gulped, wondering what she was in for. But seeing an unfamiliar car parked in their driveway derailed her thoughts. "Who is that?" she asked. Did Crystal actually have the nerve to come to her house?

"No worries," Ryan said. "I'm interviewing a house-keeper that Logan's mom recommended—one of her clients. That must be her."

Sure enough, as they got out of the car, the woman did as well—a small, slightly built woman in her fifties with dark curly hair piled on top of her head in a messy bun. Not what Taylor pictured as a housekeeper. Then again, what did she know of housekeepers?

"Bitsy Monroe?" Ryan asked the woman.

"That's me," the woman said with confidence and held out her hand.

Ryan shook it and introduced the three of them, then asked, "Are you ready to see the house?"

"Of course. Lead on."

Taylor smiled, liking the woman immediately. As Ryan

led the way up the driveway, Logan leaned down to her and whispered, "She's kind of small to be a housekeeper, isn't she?"

"Oh, I'm stronger than I look," Bitsy threw over her shoulder. "And I have excellent hearing."

"Busted," Taylor said with a laugh.

Logan winced and threw a "Sorry" in Bitsy's direction.

As Ryan opened the door, Mulligan came rushing toward them, his little tail wagging like mad. But when he saw Bitsy, he stopped dead in his tracks and growled like he did to most women.

"Sorry," Logan said. "He's wary of strangers." Glancing down at Mulligan, he said, "It's okay, buddy. Why don't we go outside while Ryan talks to Ms. Monroe."

The woman snorted. "The name's Bitsy. No one calls me Ms. Monroe."

"Uh, okay...Bitsy," Logan said, obviously thrown by the woman's forthright manner. Then he escaped with Mulligan out the back door.

Yep, Taylor definitely liked this woman.

"You know what needs to be done better than I do," Ryan said to Taylor. "Want to show her around?"

"Sure," Taylor said, and gave Bitsy a tour of the house. The woman gauged the rooms with a critical but knowing eye, and asked insightful questions.

When they finally returned to the living room where Ryan waited, Taylor gave him a discreet thumbs-up behind Bitsy's back.

"So, are you interested in working for us?" Ryan asked.

"Absolutely," Bitsy said. As they agreed on a weekly schedule and payment, plus fees for any extras her father might need like cooking and laundry, Logan came back in with a much calmer Mulligan.

Logan hung back. Taylor wasn't sure if it was to avoid the woman who'd disconcerted him or to keep Mulligan away. Probably both.

"There's just one final step," Ryan said. "I'll need to introduce you to our father, who you'll actually be working for."

"And your father is...?"

"Tommy Nash."

Bitsy grinned. "Oh, Tommy and I go way back. I used to run the booster club when he was coaching at the high school. We get along fine."

"Okay, good. Then we have a deal. You can start this coming Thursday?"

"Absolutely. Though I will need a key, in case no one's home."

"Oh, that's right." Ryan pulled one out of his pocket and gave it to her.

"What about the dog?" Bitsy asked.

"He won't be here much longer," Logan explained. "And if he is, don't worry. He'll growl, but ignore him and he'll leave you alone."

"Excellent," Bitsy said. "Any other special instructions I need to know?" she asked Taylor.

"Just that Dad doesn't like his trophy case messed with, and I'd prefer you not clean my studio—I'll do that myself."

"You got it," Bitsy said. Waving a hand in farewell, she headed confidently out the door.

"Well, that was easy," Ryan said with a sigh of relief. "I think she'll be great."

"Yeah," Logan drawled. "Dust bunnies don't have a chance with her around."

Ryan laughed. "You got that right." Then, pulling out his phone, he said, "I'd better let Dad know. Why don't you two go...practice?"

All of a sudden, Taylor felt very self-conscious again.

"Way to be subtle, Nash," Logan said with a growl. Then, turning to Taylor, he said, "Ignore him. You said you have your own studio?"

"Yes," Taylor said with relief, grateful that Logan had changed the subject. "Would you like to see it?"

"I would. I'd like to see where my money is going," he added with a grin.

Taylor led him upstairs, Mulligan trotting along behind them. "I started out working in my bedroom, but it soon overflowed. So, I took over Mom's old sewing room."

She led him to the room and opened it, trying to see it with his eyes. It was a bit crowded, but perfect for her needs with a light table, a drafting table, a small desk for her laptop, and open shelving for storage.

Logan gestured at the shelves. "What's all this?"

"The tools of my trade," Taylor said with a smile, happy to show off her business to someone who appeared interested. "I have a bunch of different kinds of paper, depending on what the client needs, plus all my pens, inks, watercolors, brushes, books, and the like."

"I had no idea it was so involved," Logan said. He wandered over to her drafting table where she had left some work to dry. "What's this?"

"It's a start on the wedding invitations Lana hired me to do. The project I hope to use to jump-start my business."

He leaned down to peer at the invitations. "Wow, I'm impressed. I had no idea you were so..."

"Competent?" she asked with a raised eyebrow. People often underestimated her.

"Well, no, I figured that. But you're really talented, and very professional." He straightened and gestured at the walls, covered with positive sayings in a variety of techniques. "Is this your work, too?"

"Yep, all of it. And you'll see it in various places around town as well. After I did the sign for the Barcelona Room, I started getting commissions from other businesses."

"I can see why."

Pleased by his obvious admiration, Taylor said, "I also teach classes occasionally at the library."

"Really? Where did *you* learn how to do this?"

She shrugged. "Oh, you know. Books, YouTube, Instagram...and practice. Lots and lots of practice. I've been doing this since high school."

"Glad to see my money is going to such an impressive operation."

"Thank you." Then, remembering what Ryan had said, she squirmed a little, but gathered her courage and said, "You've kept your side of the bargain. Now I need to keep mine."

"The practicing, you mean?" he asked softly.

"Uh, yeah." She couldn't meet his eyes, and felt a blush warm her cheeks. She must be flaming red by now.

"Where would you like to do it?"

"Not here, obviously."

"Your room?"

"No," she said quickly. The only piece of furniture there was her bed, and she felt awkward enough as it was. "The den, I think. It has a loveseat." Oh, shoot. She'd said the "L" word. He wouldn't think—

She cut her thoughts off abruptly. No, why would he? It was a perfectly appropriate name for the piece of furniture. *Stop being so squirrely,* she told herself firmly.

"Sounds good," he said.

As he left the room, she wondered about her breath. Did she have time to brush her teeth? No, that was silly. When his back was turned, she scrambled in her desk drawer and grabbed a breath mint and popped it into her mouth. He turned back to look at her and she tucked the mint in her cheek, smiling around it. *Nothing to see here.* She gestured toward the open door.

Logan went downstairs, Mulligan at his heels. Taylor followed, working the mint furiously in her mouth.

When Logan entered the den—her father's bastion of masculinity—Taylor closed the door so just the three of them were inside. Interruptions would only be more embarrassing. Logan sat on the leather loveseat and Mulligan jumped up beside him, then growled, warning Taylor away.

She hesitated, not wanting to do anything to upset the cute dog. Logan frowned down at Mulligan. "Let's try something." He stood, leaving Mulligan on the loveseat and gestured for her to come closer. "I'm going to hug you so Mulligan knows I see you as part of the family—part of my pack."

Taylor nodded, then stiffened as Logan put his arms around her.

"Relax," Logan encouraged her. "We're supposed to be engaged, remember? And Mulligan needs to think this is real as well."

Yeah, but if she relaxed, she'd start to enjoy this waaaaay too much.

He had a point, though. That was the whole purpose of this...practice. To get her comfortable with him.

Relax and enjoy it, she told herself sternly. *Just not too much.*

She let herself lean into him, though her head only came up midway on his chest. His hold was secure yet gentle, as if he feared she might break. As she relaxed, she inhaled deeply. He smelled so good—all musky and woodsy and manly. Yum.

She swallowed the rest of the mint and asked, "Now what?"

They had their heads turned toward Mulligan, who was standing on the loveseat, head tilted, looking uncertain.

"Just stay here for a few minutes. He's been responding to you more positively over the past few days, right?"

"Yeah. I've been giving him treats and respecting his space," she said into his chest. So warm....

"Sometimes he just needs a little time to get to know you, and to know you're not a danger to either of us. Let's try sitting down together."

They sat, and he kept one arm around her. There wasn't enough space for Mulligan as well, so he jumped up onto the arm of the loveseat next to Logan.

"Come here, boy," Logan said gently and patted his lap. Mulligan climbed gingerly into his lap, curled up, and looked up at Taylor with a wary expression. "No growling, that's good." Logan stroked the dog's head with his free hand and said, "Now, let him sniff your hand and see if he growls. If he doesn't, then try to pet him."

Taylor held out her hand, palm up, and Mulligan sniffed it, but didn't let out a peep, thank heavens. Logan continued to stroke his back while Taylor tentatively fondled Mulligan's silky ears. He was so cute, she'd been wanting to do this for ages, but didn't want to upset the little pup. "He's adorable," she said and glanced up at Logan.

OMG. His face was *right there*. He gave her an enigmatic expression. "Yes, adorable," he murmured then leaned down and kissed her on the forehead.

She inhaled sharply at the affectionate gesture. Trying to get it under control, she asked, "Are you trying to gentle me as much as the dog, Logan Kelly?"

"Maybe," he said with a grin. "Is it working?"

"I think so." She certainly felt more comfortable with him now, though she was still afraid to let her feelings show.

"Good." He kissed her nose. "There, that's not so bad, is it?"

She smiled. "No." Though it wasn't exactly what Ryan had in mind....

"Okay, now you kiss me," Logan said softly. She drew away a little, alarmed. "My cheek, I mean."

Okay, that was doable. He leaned down and offered her his cheek. She pecked it quickly and he withdrew.

"Okay, now let's do the other cheek and try not to act like you'll burn your lips if you linger."

Well, he *was* totally hot....

He turned his other cheek toward her, and she kissed it like she would her father's.

"Much better," Logan approved. "Now try it again."

He offered her his other cheek again, but when she went to kiss it, he turned his head so their lips met instead.

Frozen in surprise, Taylor didn't pull away, but let herself enjoy the movement of his lips against hers for a lovely moment.

He withdrew to gaze down at her. Taylor could do nothing but stare at him, desperately hoping he'd continue, yet afraid he would at the same time. *Come on, Taylor. Pull up your big girl panties and do this.*

He leaned down again, slowly, giving her a chance to pull away, but she met him halfway and he kissed her lips exploringly, then deepened it into the most achingly tender kiss she'd ever received. Her limbs felt as if they'd liquified, and she was glad they weren't still standing, or she'd probably fall into a puddle on the floor.

His other arm came around her and she vaguely realized Mulligan had jumped down. Leaning into the kiss, she slid her arm up around his neck.

Oh, my. As if they had a mind of their own, her lips parted, and he delved inside, searching, seeking for...something. She didn't know what it was, but she gave him everything, letting her feelings show for the first time ever.

Drawing back to take a breath, she looked up at him searchingly. Her heart beat so fast, she was afraid it would leap out of her chest. Did he know? Could he tell how she felt?

He bent his head, dropping warm kisses against her neck. "You okay?" he murmured.

Unable to speak while sensations zinged through her, she nodded wordlessly.

"Then let's make this a little easier." He picked her up and slid her onto his lap. His arms tight around her, he leaned in, saying, "Let's try that again."

She put her arms around his neck and he proceeded to kiss her senseless. Lost in a sea of overwhelming sensation, she forgot that she didn't want him to know how she felt, and just leaned into it with her whole heart, shutting out the rest of the world.

But the world intruded when she heard a loud clearing of a throat and realized it wasn't the first time she'd heard that sound. She drew away and saw her father standing there, grinning at them.

How long had he been standing there? Scrambling off Logan's lap, she covered her flaming cheeks with her hands. "Dad, we were just, er—" Just what? She couldn't tell him they were practicing.

Her father chuckled. "I'm not so old that I can't tell what you were doing. But maybe you could do it somewhere else? I need to use my computer."

"Of course," Taylor said, deliberately not looking at Logan. She fled the room, hoping she wouldn't die of mortification.

Challenge accepted? No, challenge *nailed*. First round to Logan.

CHAPTER EIGHT

THE NEXT DAY, Logan came downstairs for breakfast, wondering which Taylor Nash he'd find. The prickly one who seemed to be annoyed by everything he did, or the pliable one he'd kissed on the loveseat yesterday? He hoped it was the latter. The "practice" had been unexpectedly enjoyable. No, that was too tame a word. He'd forgotten they were there simply to ease her nervousness and make their deception more believable...and just lost himself in her. He didn't remember ever having felt like that with anyone else before. *And why did I wait so long?* he wondered.

Unfortunately, she'd disappeared after her father caught them necking and hadn't come down at all after that. He hoped she wasn't too mortified. Would she even be at breakfast?

Smelling bacon, he followed his nose to the kitchen where Taylor was cooking for her father and brother, looking adorable in jeans and a pretty blue top. Taylor glanced at him quickly, then concentrated on the pan in front of her.

No way was he going to let her put distance between

them. Grinning to himself, he walked over to the stove and put his arms around her. When she turned around in surprise, he dropped a brief kiss on her lips. "Good morning, sweetheart."

She stiffened then glanced at her father, obviously thinking he'd done it for Coach's benefit. Nope, it was all for him, though she didn't need to know that.

"Good morning," she replied, sounding a little breathy. "I'm uh, making scrambled eggs and bacon. Want some?"

"I'd love that, thanks."

He moved away to pour himself a cup of coffee and fix Mulligan's breakfast.

"Good morning," Coach said heartily. "Sleep well?"

Logan nodded. "Thank you so much for letting me stay here."

"No problem. After all, you're going to be family soon."

Logan smiled at the man's obvious delight. "That's right."

"Have you decided what you're going to do now that you're retired from the game?"

Logan shrugged. "I haven't really had time to think about it." What with getting engaged and kissing practice and all. He set Mulligan's food in front of the eager dog and sat at the table.

"Well, Hal's been having a bit of a rough time keeping the golf course profitable. After you left yesterday, we got to talking and thought maybe you'd be interested in being the golf pro there."

"Teaching? I'm not sure I can do that until my shoulder is healed."

"Oh, sure you can. You don't have to swing a club yourself—just advise others on their game until your shoulder heals. And, honestly, just having your name associated with the club will help a lot."

"I'll think about it," Logan said. Did he still want to stay in golf? It was all he really knew, but he kind of wanted to do something more important with his life.

Taylor slid a plate in front of him and added some scrambled egg to Mulligan's dish. Mulligan gave her hand a lick and dug in.

"Are you trying to spoil my dog?" Logan asked teasingly, though he was glad Mulligan had obviously warmed to her.

"Guilty," she said, sliding into a seat with her own plate. "I miss having a dog."

"Well, you can spoil Mulligan all you like."

Ryan glanced up from his phone. "Have you seen the latest from that golf gossip website?"

Dread filled him. "No. Now what?"

"It's from that reporter who cornered you at the restaurant. It's easier if I just read it to all of you."

When Ryan finished, Logan frowned in annoyance. The man had reported his retirement factually enough, but then veered into yellow journalism with his reporting of Logan and Taylor's engagement, hinting broadly that there was something iffy about the whole thing since neither Logan nor Taylor would talk to him. Obviously, the idiot had been talking to Crystal.

"There's a picture, too," Ryan said, and showed them one of Taylor looking surprised in Logan's arms, with Crystal, her eyes wide, looking on in disbelief. The reporter must have taken it without them noticing.

"Oh, great," Taylor said. "I look awful after a full day at work, and Crystal looks great."

"You didn't look awful," Logan protested. Then, remembering Coach's presence, he added, "You always look beautiful to me."

She rolled her eyes at him as her father frowned down at the article. "Want me to set him straight?" Coach asked.

"No," Logan said. "It'll just add more fuel to the fire. I'll ask Mom to make an announcement to the paper." He should have thought of that before.

"Okay," Coach said as he got to his feet. "I've got to get to work. Think about that golf pro job, won't you?"

"I will," Logan promised.

After he left, Ryan said, "So what are we going to do about this?"

Logan sighed. "What can we do? It's not like he's wrong. Besides, the only one we really need to convince is Crystal."

"And the other groupies," Ryan reminded him.

"And the town," Taylor added. "Especially since Crystal essentially said the town didn't believe we were engaged."

Ryan nodded. "After this, I bet we get more tabloid reporters coming to Dogwood to see if they can find juicy details."

"Well, we have to convince Dogwood, then," Taylor said, seeming fired up about the whole thing.

Logan regarded her with a smile. "How are we going to do that?"

A slow smile spread across her face. "By using Dogwood's fastest means of spreading the news—gossip."

"Yes," Ryan crowed. "Give those busybodies something to talk about. Heck, Dad and Logan's mom will start it—you just need to corroborate it." Then, in a change of subject, he asked, "How did the kissing practice go?"

Taylor looked a little rattled, so Logan answered for her. "Fine. So, what are you saying, Ryan? That we need to..." he searched for a word that wouldn't offend her, "canoodle in public?"

Taylor gave him a disbelieving glance. "Canoodle? Really?"

Well, the word had distracted her, as he intended. He shrugged.

"Yes," Ryan said. "The biggest gossips are Irene Harrington and Janice Carter. Do they still have lunch most days at the Blossom Café?"

"So far as I know," Taylor said.

"Then you know what you gotta do."

Logan nodded. "You up for putting our practice to work...in public?"

She chewed on her lower lip. "You think it'll work?"

"You bet it will," Ryan said. "Then, when the other reporters come, they'll only hear *your* side of the story from the townspeople. Besides, don't you want to stick it to Crystal?"

Taylor shot Ryan a look that Logan couldn't decipher. "Okay, let's do it," she said.

If she was up for more practice, who was he to stand in her way? "I have that physical therapy appointment at ten," he reminded her. "Want to meet at the café after that? Say, about 11:30?"

"Prime gossip time," Ryan said in approval.

"Sounds good," Taylor said. "That'll give me some time to work on the wedding invitations first."

Several hours later, Logan had finished with his therapy and had some time to kill, so he wandered into Betty's Flowers, wanting to do something nice for Taylor.

He walked over to the refrigerated case where the roses were. "Can I help you find something?" the woman behind the counter asked.

"Yes, I'm meeting my fiancée for lunch today." And didn't that sound odd coming out of his mouth? "I want to get her something special."

72

"Is this for a special occasion or just because?"

He couldn't tell her the truth—that he wanted to make their engagement appear more real for the gossips, so he said, "Just because."

"Red roses signify love and passion, and are probably more appropriate for a special occasion," the woman said. "But we have an excellent selection of other flowers. What's her favorite color?"

He had no clue. But he did remember that sweater she wore yesterday. "Pink, I think."

"And what kind of personality does she have? Would she like something classic and timeless, or modern and unique?"

How would he know? "Uh, well, she's spunky and smart, and she does calligraphy, so she's creative...."

"Calligraphy? Is this for Taylor Nash?"

"Yes, you know her?" He didn't know why he was so surprised—this was a relatively small town.

"Yes, she did the lettering on my front window. I didn't know she was engaged."

"It just happened yesterday."

"Congratulations. And I know exactly what she would like. Do you trust me?"

"Uh, sure."

"You want a vase, too, I take it?"

"Whatever you think is best," Logan said with relief, glad to have the decision taken out of his hands.

"Do you want to take it now, or have it delivered?"

He'd feel silly carrying a bunch of flowers around. "Well, I need it for lunch today at the Blossom Café down the street. Do you think you can make the arrangement right away and help me surprise her by delivering them there a little after 11:30?"

"Of course."

"Perfect."

He paid for the flowers, and strolled down to the café to wait for Taylor, though he was a little early.

He chose a booth about midway in the café where everyone could see them, and hoped the two gossips were there. It had been a long time since he'd spent much time in town around the locals, so he wouldn't recognize them on sight.

He ordered a soda, but Taylor didn't keep him waiting long. Exactly at 11:30, she came in and had obviously dressed up for the occasion, in a soft, flowy dress in pastel colors that looked like something from an impressionist's painting. She'd put on makeup and done something to her hair, too, to make her look sultry. It was the most feminine he'd ever seen her. Though he wished she'd done this just for him, he knew it was because of their role-playing.

"Taylor, over here," he called out, deliberately loud.

As she made her way to the booth, he stood and leaned down and kissed her, saying, "You look beautiful."

Conversation stopped in the café as everyone turned to look at them. Taylor's cheeks were a little pink, but she slid into the booth. Instead of sitting across from her, Logan slid in beside her. She looked a little surprised, but that's what a real fiancé would do, right?

The waitress showed up right away, curiosity plain on her face. "Hi, Taylor. Can I get you something to drink?"

"Iced tea, please."

When the waitress looked pointedly at Logan, Taylor added, "Tina, this is my fiancé, Logan Kelly. Logan, this is Tina. We've known each other forever."

Tina gaped. "Fiancé? Is that your ring?"

"Yes," Taylor said with a smile and held it out so Tina could admire it.

"Gorgeous," Tina said. "I can't believe you're engaged. I didn't even know you were dating."

Curling Taylor's fingers in his on top of the table, Logan said, "We wanted to keep it quiet while I was still...working, but now we can shout it to the world."

"Oh, my," Tina said. "Congratulations."

"Thank you."

Tina hurried off, presumably to tell everyone she knew about their engagement.

Logan bent his head to whisper to Taylor as if he was sharing something private. "Are the gossips here?" he asked softly.

She nodded. "They're two booths in front of us—and staring like we're a zoo exhibit."

"Perfect." He picked up the menu. "It's been a while since I've been here. What's good?"

"Just about everything."

Tina returned then and took their order. Taylor ordered a salad, and Logan ordered their daily special—a patty melt and fries.

"Right away," Tina said. She headed back toward the kitchen, but one of the gossips snagged her. They whispered and looked in Taylor's direction.

He suppressed a smile. "Looks like it's working."

"I think so."

The café door opened then, and a teenager stood surveying the restaurant. "Taylor Nash?" he called. "Delivery for Taylor Nash."

Looking stunned, Taylor raised her hand. "That's me," she squeaked.

The boy strode toward her. "Then these are for you."

He set the flowers on the table—a beautiful arrangement of pastel flowers that arched in an elegant curve over a low white pottery vase. It kind of matched the colors in her dress.

Turning a delighted face to Logan, she asked, "Did you do this?"

He nodded. "I wanted to do something special for you." He lowered his voice. "To thank you for doing this for me."

"You didn't have to do that," she protested, but the delight on her face showed it was the perfect thing to do.

And if everyone's eyes hadn't been on them before, they certainly were now. "Yes, I did," he said, kissing her fingers. "I wanted you to have something as beautiful as you to look at."

She smiled, but murmured, "Coming on a bit strong, aren't you?"

He'd actually meant it, but sensed she wouldn't inter- ested in hearing that. "No," he whispered back. "They're eating it up."

"Well, thank you. No matter what the reason, they're absolutely stunning." She lifted her mouth to kiss him—the first kiss she'd actually initiated.

He couldn't help it—he gave her a long, lingering one. Not for the benefit of the spectators, but just because he liked kissing her. "There, that wasn't so bad, was it?"

She shook her head, and the whispers started up. Mission accomplished.

Taylor ignored them to ask how his physical therapy had gone. Relieved that she seemed to be more comfort- able with him, he told her about the appointment, and they chatted about everything under the sun as they ate lunch.

As they walked out of the restaurant hand in hand for the benefit of the gossips, Taylor carrying her flowers, he asked, "Do you think that worked?"

"You bet it did. Did you see how Irene and Janice hurried out of there? I betcha the whole town knows by dinnertime." She halted suddenly, staring at a woman walking a border collie mix. "Let's go a different way." She turned around and hurried off, tugging him to keep up with her.

"What's that all about?"

"That dog—that's the new Match."

"Oh, the matchmaking dog?" He hadn't met the newest incarnation of Match, who had a far better track record of bringing soul mates together than any dating app.

"Yeah. We don't want to meet Match when we're together, so she doesn't expose our deception."

He glanced back at the dog. "Uh-oh."

"What?" she asked. "Is she coming this way?"

"No, but Crystal is talking to the woman walking Match." And he could swear the dog was staring at them and laughing....

CHAPTER NINE

On cloud nine, Taylor beat Logan home, and floated into the house with her flowers. At least, that's how it felt. The lunch was excellent, the company was sublime, and it had felt so wonderful to be with Logan. He was so attentive, so sweet.... And the flowers? Utterly gorgeous. How nice of him to think of it.

And the kissing practice yesterday... She shook her head. She had no words superlative enough. Why had she been so nervous? He'd made her feel comfortable, and kissed her as if she were the only person on earth. Could he really kiss her like that and have no feelings for her?

Ryan, with Mulligan in his lap, sat in the living room where she placed the flowers on an end table—the perfect place to show them off. "Nice," he exclaimed. "Where did those come from?"

"Logan bought them for me." She touched one pale petal, marveling at the beauty of the arrangement.

Logan came in as Ryan said, "Oh, I see. The flowers were to keep up the pretense."

"That's right, buddy," Logan said.

Her heart fell. *Way to prick my bubble, Ryan.* She turned her face away so they wouldn't see her disappointment.

"Did it work?" Ryan asked.

"Taylor said the gossips were both there, so I think so," Logan answered absently as he leaned down to pet the ecstatic Mulligan.

Ryan clapped him on the back. "Good thinking. With any luck, this will help get rid of Crystal. Bet you'll be glad when she's gone and this is all over."

"You got that right," Logan said.

Pain stabbed through her chest. "Excuse me," Taylor said, and ran up to her room before they could see the anguish on her face.

Closing the bedroom door, she leaned against it and covered her mouth to bite back a sob. For one lovely hour or so, she'd forgotten about the fake engagement, forgotten that Logan was just being kind to her in order to scare another woman off. But as Logan and Ryan had just so baldly reminded her, it was all a sham. And that's all it would ever be.

Tears streamed down her face at the memory of Logan saying he'd be glad when this was all over. Stupid. She was stupid for believing any of it could be real. She'd just have to remember this whole thing was a lie while she kept Logan from realizing she wished it wasn't.

A knock came at the door. "What?" she asked, her voice thick.

"It's me," Logan said. "Can I come in?"

"Uh, just a minute," Taylor said, and grabbed a handful of tissues to frantically wipe away her tears. Glancing in the mirror, she saw her eyes and nose were red. Darn it—he'd know she'd been crying. Well, it couldn't be helped.

Composing herself and reminding herself not to be a fool, Taylor said, "Come in."

The door opened just wide enough for her to see Mulligan's head peek in, at about the height of her shoulder. Logan followed tentatively, holding the dog. "Mulligan was worried about you. Are you all right?"

"I'm fine," she said shortly.

Logan looked down at Mulligan. "What's that, boy?" He bent down as if listening to the dog speak, and glanced at Taylor. "He says you don't look fine."

Cute. Smiling at his silliness, she said, "Maybe, but tell him I will be."

She sank down on the bed and he joined her there, the dog between them. Mulligan laid his paw on her arm and looked up at her with what she swore was a concerned expression. Did he sense she was upset? She patted the dog's paw in reassurance.

"What's wrong?" Logan asked softly. "You know I only meant that I'll be glad to get rid of Crystal, right?"

"I know," she lied and gestured helplessly. She couldn't tell him the whole truth, but she could tell him part of it. "It's just that it...got to me."

"The pretending?"

She nodded. "Lying to my friends, our families...it's hard not to feel guilty. What will they think when we finally tell them the truth?" She stared down at the tissues in her hand, and told herself to stop shredding them.

"We don't have to," Logan said. "We can just 'break up' and they'll think I'm an idiot for letting you go."

Even now, he was being so sweet, it made her heart ache. "More likely the other way around," she muttered.

"Well, tell you what. Why don't we do something together tomorrow where we're not under a magnifying glass, we don't have to pretend, and can just be ourselves."

That would be nice for a change. "Like what?"

"I'm not sure. Do you have any ideas?"

She thought for a minute. "Well, the Dogwood Express is returning tomorrow afternoon to Sanctuary with a with a bunch of puppy mill dogs who will need special treatment. They always need help in processing the dogs, but it can take awhile. Would you like to do that?"

Logan glanced down at the dog between them. "Mulligan thinks that's an excellent idea...and so do I. Do you know what time?"

"Not exactly. They'll post the arrival time on Facebook and Twitter, so we'll know when to arrive."

"Okay, sounds like a plan."

❖ ❖ ❖ ❖

THE NEXT DAY, Taylor wrestled her emotions under control as they drove to Sanctuary. They arrived just as the Dogwood Express bus was pulling in, and, as they got out of the car, Logan asked, "What do we do?"

"They'll unload the bus and give each dog to a volunteer. Basically, you hold onto them and make them feel loved as they go through the intake process."

"Make them feel loved?"

"Yes—many of these dogs come from puppy mills where they've been used to produce litter after litter to sell, and their living conditions are horrendous. Others are cast-offs, strays, or simply unwanted litters. Most of them have never felt any kindness from a human before."

He frowned. "That's awful."

They went to stand in line, and she said, "Warning: they can be rather dirty."

"That's why you told me to wear old clothes?"

She nodded and went to stand in the crowd outside the bus, where Sandy and Paul McPherson, the owners and operators of the Sanctuary rescue, were assuring each volunteer got a dog.

Taylor stepped up to the bus and smiled as they handed her a Maltese terrier and put a slip leash over the dog's head. Though Maltese dogs normally had soft, long white hair, this one's hair was almost gray—ungroomed and matted. When Taylor took her in her arms, the dog trembled in fear. *Poor little thing.* Taylor wrapped her arms around the dog and tried to beam love and reassurance from her heart into the dog's.

Logan was up next, and they handed him a Jack Russell terrier. He took the dog gently and followed Taylor inside where they started the intake process. As they stood in line, waiting for the first station, Logan glanced down at the dog. "He's really calm for a Jack Russell. Every one I've ever seen before has been bouncing off the walls, full of energy."

"Probably due to the conditions in which he was living."

Logan nodded and his jaw clenched. "People who abuse animals ought to be shot."

The older man in front of them said, "You got that right. Or be forced to live in the same conditions where they keep these poor little guys." He went on to describe the filthy, crowded wire cages where the dogs were kept without access to veterinary care, groomers, or proper nutrition. "Most have never even seen sunlight or felt grass under their paws," he went on to say, tears glinting in his eyes. "The Sanctuary folks are true heroes, for taking care of these mistreated animals and finding them loving homes. That's why I've been volunteering here for so long."

Obviously interested, Logan asked the man to elaborate on what Sanctuary did, since he had been gone so long from the town. As the man, who identified himself as Hugh Strong, did that, Taylor tuned them out. She was already familiar with the wonderful things Sanctuary did, so she spent her time cuddling the little Maltese. "You'll be okay, sweetie," she crooned. "They'll find you a wonderful home where you'll finally feel the love you deserve." The sweet little girl had stopped trembling and looked up at Taylor as she spoke, then rested her head against Taylor's chest as if she finally felt safe.

Hugh turned away to speak to someone else, and Logan turned back to her, stroking the little terrier in his arms. "Looks like you need to get a dog of your own, Taylor."

She shook her head. "I want one, but Dad has had too much loss, what with losing Mom then our dog. I need to wait until he's ready again." She smiled at him. "I think Mulligan's helping with that."

Logan smiled. "Yeah, I caught the two of them snoring on the couch together last night, Mulligan laying on your father's chest."

The first station called them up, and they went together. Amber McPherson, the honey-blond daughter of the owners—and one of Taylor's best friends—was there, of course. "So glad to see you," Amber said, giving Taylor a hug. "We hardly get to see each other anymore."

"I know, but you've been a bit busy with your fiancé. Where is Dillon, anyway?"

"Oh, he's taking pictures of the dogs today at another station," Amber said. "And now you have a fiancé too. Is this him?"

Knowing it was impossible to get away from *all* mentions of their fake engagement, Taylor nodded and introduced Logan and Amber. Besides, she knew Amber wouldn't pry, especially since they couldn't talk long in line.

After she recorded the basics for each dog, Amber asked, "And what do you want to name them?"

Logan frowned. "They don't have names?"

"No," Amber said with a sigh. "The puppy mills only give them numbers, so we give them a name when they arrive. Their new parents might give them a different one after they're adopted, but at least they won't be treated like faceless numbers while they're here."

"I see," Logan said, and looked down at the terrier assessingly. "I think he looks like a Bogey."

"Okay," Taylor said. "To keep with the theme, maybe mine should be named Lauren."

When Logan looked at her in puzzlement, she added, "You know, Lauren Bacall. She and Humphrey Bogart were married."

The light dawned on his face. "Oh, I didn't mean the actor. I was thinking that since I named Mulligan after a golf term, I ought to do the same for this one. You know...one stroke over par. A bogey."

Of course. Now she felt dumb. "Oh, duh. Then let's call this one Birdie."

"Bogey and Birdie it is," Amber said, then handed them each a folder with the dogs' information inside. "I hope we can get together soon."

"Thanks," Taylor said, standing. "Our parents are throwing an engagement party, and you're invited, of course."

"Sounds great," Amber said, and they moved on.

They spent the next couple of hours moving through the process to get the dogs' weight, check for microchips, get their pictures taken, and have a veterinary checkup with vaccinations and deworming, among other things.

They took the dogs out to do their business, and both dogs stepped a little gingerly on the grass. "They've probably never seen grass before," Taylor said sadly. "They've only had wire cages beneath their feet with nothing soft to cushion them."

"I can see why you volunteer here," Logan said. "Hugh was right—these people are heroes."

"Not heroes," a man said behind her. "Just animal lovers trying to make life a little better for those who have been mistreated." He stuck out his hand. "Hi, I'm Paul McPherson, owner of this place, along with my wife, Sandy."

"He's Amber's father," Taylor explained.

Logan shook his hand. "Logan Kelly. I just moved back to town, and Taylor brought me with her today."

Moved back? Meaning he was here to stay? She could only hope....

"We're glad to have all of our volunteers," Paul said.

"You do good work," Logan said. "Do you mind if I ask you a few more questions?"

"Of course not."

They went back to sit in the comfortable chairs in the waiting room donated by the fire department, where Logan quizzed Paul about how Sanctuary worked.

"Not much longer," Taylor told Birdie, stroking the dog in her lap. "You'll soon have a soft bed and good food. Maybe even toys. Does that sound good?"

The little dog just looked at her in puzzlement, probably unable to comprehend the thought of such luxury. Taylor looked over at Logan, absentmindedly petting Bogey as he spoke to Paul about how Sanctuary operated. She'd always been attracted to Logan, not only for his looks, but because of his kindness to her when he'd probably thought of her as Ryan's bratty little sister. But she was learning more and more about him every day. Compassionate with people and animals, a good sense of humor, a great listener, and a world-class golfer who was generous with his time and money...he was the total package. She had wondered if she would get tired of having him around all the time, but no, she just wanted more. Taylor sighed inwardly. She was in trouble, especially if he did stay in town. Sooner or later, he was going to realize she was in love with him, and hire someone else to get rid of *her*.

Don't be ridiculous, she told herself. He wouldn't do that. They'd been friends too long. He'd try to let her down gently. She winced. That might be even worse. Not for the first time, she wondered...was it even possible he would finally see how right they were for each other?

Yeah, right.

Saddened by the thought, she wondered how much time she had left with him. It didn't matter—it wouldn't be enough, no matter how much she had. So...why was she fighting it? Why was she trying to keep him at arm's length? To heck with that. From now on, she was going to enjoy this brief time they had together, and try not to think about the future or the consequences.

"Where is he?" came a strident voice behind her. "I know he's here. I saw his car."

Taylor peered around the tall chair. Through the open door, she saw Crystal in one of her sausage-casing dresses, berating Sandy at the front desk.

Taylor pulled her head back swiftly and glanced at Logan, wondering if he'd heard.

Yep. He closed his eyes in resignation. "I can't believe she found me here."

Paul rose and patted Logan on the shoulder. "No problem. I can take care of this."

With their backs to the door, the chairs were tall enough that Crystal wouldn't be able to see them if they remained still. They could still hear the entire conversation though.

Paul asked, "Is there a problem here?"

"No problem," Crystal cooed, sounding as if she was trying to seduce Paul now. "I'm just looking for my boyfriend, Logan Kelly."

"Boyfriend?" Logan mouthed to Taylor in disbelief.

Taylor shook her head, mystified by Crystal's persistence in pursuing someone who obviously wasn't interested in her.

"I'm sorry, he's busy," Paul said. "Everyone here has their hands full processing rescue dogs."

"But he'll want to see me," Crystal persisted.

"The only way we can let you in at this time is if you plan to carry a dog through the intake process."

"But they're so...dirty," Crystal said, disgust in her voice.

"Then I'm sorry," Paul said. "You can't come in."

Taylor risked a peek around the chair. Crystal clenched her hands into fists. "If you don't let me see him, I—I'll sue you," she threatened.

Sandy spoke up. "You can try, but we reserve the right to refuse service to anyone. You're not welcome here. If you don't leave now, you'll be considered a trespasser, and I'll call the sheriff."

Paul nodded. "And he just happens to be my cousin."

Crystal made an inarticulate sound of rage and stomped out the door.

Go, Sandy!

"Are they really cousins?" Logan whispered.

"Of some sort, I'm sure. All the McPhersons are related in some way or another. They founded the town, remember?"

Paul came back in and Logan told him, "Thanks—you don't know how much I appreciate that."

"No problem. I made sure she drove off, and Sandy

wasn't kidding. She isn't welcome around here, and we'll have her arrested for trespassing if she shows up again."

"Maybe we should stay here until she leaves town," Taylor joked.

His expression wry, Logan merely nodded. "Not a bad idea." He glanced down at Bogey. "Care to share your bed, little guy?"

Paul chuckled. "I don't think it would be big enough for you."

One of the volunteers called for them then, to finalize the process and settle the dogs in their temporary home.

As they were leaving, Paul came up to them. "Logan, if you want to know more about our operation, just give me a call." He handed Logan a business card.

Logan tucked it in his shirt pocket. "Thanks. I will."

"What was that all about?" Taylor asked as they walked to the car. Luckily, Crystal was long gone, as Paul had promised.

Logan shrugged. "They do good work. I was just wondering how I could help."

What a nice guy.

"Besides," he added, "he helped us get rid of Crystal. I owe him one."

Taylor sighed as she settled herself in the car. "She seems so determined. What's up with that?"

"I have no idea."

"I mean, she's like a dog worrying a bone. Why does she want you so badly, anyway?"

He took his eyes off the road for a moment to quirk an eyebrow at her. "Is it so hard to believe a woman would find me attractive?"

"Of course not." But to keep him from getting a big head, she teased, "You're...adequate-looking."

He looked as though he wasn't sure whether to be affronted or amused.

"But most women would have taken the hint by now and left. Did you date her? Give her some encouragement? Before you got here, I mean."

"No," he said vehemently. "I was polite on the tour, but she seemed to see that as a come-on. I've been dodging her at the last three tournaments."

"Then what's her deal? What makes her so persistent?"

Logan frowned. "I don't know. It does seem strange, doesn't it?"

"It does," Taylor said firmly. "Maybe we should do some research on *her* for a change and try to figure out why she's after you."

Logan nodded thoughtfully. "Good idea. Maybe if we know why she wants me so badly, we can get rid of her once and for all."

"Yeah," Taylor said, then realized that, by doing so, she'd shorten her time with Logan. *Great move, genius* she thought sarcastically. Remembering her vow to enjoy their time together, no matter how short, she glanced at him speculatively as he parked in their driveway.

"What's that look mean?" he asked.

She gathered her courage, though her heart was pounding to beat the drum. "Well, to convince Crystal to leave, I'm thinking...maybe I need a little more practice."

Both his eyebrows went up and his mouth opened as if in shock, but that didn't last long. Almost immediately, he grinned. "Happy to oblige," he said, then leaned over to kiss her.

Her heart leapt wildly as he gave her a brief kiss, and, when he would have pulled away, she snaked her hand to the back of his head and held him there, needing more....

He deepened the kiss until there was nothing left in the universe except Logan, his incredible mouth, and—

A knock at the driver's side window had them jerking apart.

Ryan peered in. "What's going on?" he asked with a frown.

Uh-oh. Big brother did not look amused.

CHAPTER TEN

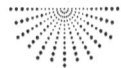

LOGAN LOWERED THE WINDOW, with absolutely no idea how to respond to Ryan. He'd just been caught making out with his best friend's little sister, something he'd vowed not to do since they were kids and it had become clear Ryan was very protective of Taylor.

But Taylor had no problem with providing a comeback. "We're practicing, Ryan. What does it look like?" When Ryan's frown didn't abate, she added, "You told us to, remember?"

"Yeah, but I didn't think you'd enjoy it so much," he muttered.

Too bad. Logan didn't regret it, not in the least.

Ryan persisted. "And why are you practicing out here where everyone can see you?"

"Isn't that the point?" Taylor asked.

Logan got out of the car, his mind darting, searching for something to remove that frown from Ryan's face. "We thought Crystal was watching. She's everywhere I go. She even showed up at Sanctuary."

Taylor had exited from the car as well. "Yeah," she said,

giving him a look he found hard to interpret. Part amused, part smug, part...he didn't know what. All he knew was that it made him want to kiss that look off her face and never stop.

Good grief. What was happening to him? He hadn't expected to enjoy this deception quite so much, but now that the spark had ignited, he wanted to pursue it further. Much further.

Ryan glanced around. "I don't see her anywhere."

Forcing his wayward hormones to behave, Logan said, "My mistake. But, speaking of Crystal, we have something to ask you. Do you have any idea *why* she's so persistent? Any other sane woman would've given up by now."

"You're assuming Crystal is sane..." Taylor muttered.

"Does it matter why?" Ryan asked Logan.

"It might. If we knew her motivation, we might be able to find some way to get rid of her. You have a lot of contacts on the tour and in the caddy community, and you keep in touch more than I do. Think you might be able to find out why she's pursuing me so hard?"

Ryan glanced between Logan and Taylor, looking suspicious. "Maybe."

"Can you try?" Logan asked. "I'm getting really tired of her showing up everywhere I go. Plus, the inquiries would be better coming from you than from me."

"Okay," Ryan said. "I'll try." Though his tone said he didn't think he'd learn anything.

But did Logan really want to get rid of Crystal so soon? Once he did, there would be no more kissing practice....

Taylor headed toward the front door. "I need to finish those invitations. See you later."

To head off any more questions from Ryan, Logan said, "Good idea." Then, to Ryan, he added, "While you investigate Crystal, I promised Mulligan a walk in the park. See you later."

Ryan frowned, but Logan ignored him as he retrieved the dog and loaded him in the car to go to Memorial Park. Though he'd used it as an excuse to get away from Ryan, he had to admit that he should do this more often for Mulligan's sake. "You won't tell anyone this was a pretext, will you, boy?" Logan asked as the dog enthusiastically jumped out of the car and started sniffing everything in sight.

As Logan headed down a path to the river, his mind wandered back to that kiss in the car. Unpredictable Taylor was unlike any woman he had ever dated. She had the unique ability to surprise him, to make him feel like a teenager again, hormones blazing front and center with heart-pounding exhilaration.

And, he realized, there was a great deal of satisfaction in the fact that she'd actually initiated the kiss for once. It was strange how very right this felt. Maybe because he'd daydreamed about it often after that almost-kiss years ago. Hmm. Had that daydreaming teenager within him somehow prompted him to choose Taylor to play the part of his fiancée? A subconscious wish fulfillment? Maybe. Probably, if he were honest with himself.

Unfortunately, when he got rid of Crystal, he and Taylor would have no further reason to continue this fake engagement. He frowned at the thought. Maybe not, but why couldn't they continue some kind of relationship anyway?

Then again, how would Ryan feel about it? Logan had assumed Ryan would be totally on board with it since the fake engagement was his idea, but would he continue to do so if it became real? Logan didn't want to lose Ryan's friendship, but he didn't want to lose Taylor either....

As he and Mulligan continued their walk, Logan

pondered how to turn this sham relationship into a real one...without alienating his best friend. Though his mind played with a number of possibilities, he hadn't come up with anything brilliant by the time he returned to the car. Lost in thought, he wasn't paying any attention to his surroundings until Mulligan stopped short and growled.

Logan glanced up and groaned. Crystal stood by his car, holding on to the collar of a black-and-white border collie mix who had a heart-shaped black spot on her white chest. This was a different look for Crystal—she had on skintight jeans and a pink sweater that had to be two sizes too small. He'd never seen her in anything besides revealing dresses before. Was this a new ploy of some kind?

Oh. Of course it was. It was similar to the outfit Taylor had worn the other day. Was Crystal seriously trying to emulate Taylor?

Using Mulligan's threatening growl as an excuse to stay as far as he could away from her, Logan said, "What are you doing here?"

Crystal beamed at him, holding tight to the dog's collar, though the dog was trying to squirm out of Crystal's hold. "I wanted to see you, of course." She frowned down at the border collie. "Do you know about Match?"

Oh, yeah, that was the dog Taylor had pointed out to him earlier. "What are you doing with Match? Did you steal her?"

"No, of course not. I heard about Match, and I just...borrowed her, to prove to you that we're meant to be together. You know that Match brings soul mates together, right?"

"I've heard," he said, his voice clipped. Hard to live in Dogwood for any length of time without hearing about the matchmaking dog. He'd been skeptical as a kid, but had heard too many success stories to totally dismiss it. In any case, he wasn't worried. Match looked almost as uncomfortable around Crystal as Mulligan did.

"See," Crystal said, struggling to hold on to the squirming dog, "she's here together with both of us, so we must belong together."

"That's not how it works," Logan said dryly, then bent over to pick up Mulligan to soothe the dog and ensure him he'd be safe.

"Match," someone exclaimed. "There you are." A woman darted over to Crystal. "That's my dog. Let go of her," she said with a glare at Crystal.

Yep, that was the woman he'd seen with Match the other day.

Crystal did, reluctantly. "I just wanted to prove that Logan and I are destined to be together."

The woman looked at Logan with a frown. He held out his hand. "Hi, I'm Logan Kelly. This wasn't my idea. And *she* doesn't understand how this works," he said with a jerk of his head toward Crystal.

Match glued herself to her owner's side, giving Crystal a narrow-eyed stare. The woman shook his hand, saying, "Bliss McPherson."

"How *does* it work then?" Crystal asked. She didn't bother introducing herself.

Logan petted Mulligan in his arms to keep the dog calm and said, "Would you explain?" he asked Bliss. "If you wouldn't mind?" He gave her a beseeching look, hoping she'd understand his plea to get rid of Crystal.

Bliss nodded. "Well, several times a year, at festivals and other gatherings, people can ask Match to find their true love, or confirm that two people are soul mates. Her reaction makes it pretty obvious if she thinks the two belong together. Or not." She glanced down fondly at the dog.

"She's also been known to bring couples together at random times throughout the year. She's never been wrong yet," she said with pride.

"Oh good," Crystal said. "Can you make her prove Logan and I are meant to be together?"

Logan rolled his eyes. Clueless.

"I don't *make* her do anything," Bliss said in annoyance. "Match just has a sixth sense for these things. *She* decides." She glanced down at the dog. "Match, are these two meant to be together?"

Match curled her lip and growled at Crystal. "Guess not," Bliss said with a laugh. She patted the dog. "Good girl." Obviously, she approved of Match's sentiment.

"Thank you," Logan said. "I really appreciate it."

"No problem," Bliss said, then glared at Crystal. "But next time, ask before you take someone's dog." Bliss attached a leash to Match's collar and said, "Come on, girl. Let's go."

As Bliss and Match walked away, Crystal tossed her hair. "Well, obviously, that dog doesn't have a clue. Who cares what a dog thinks, anyway?"

"I do," Logan said. He glanced down at Mulligan who still rumbled an occasional low growl at Crystal. "*My* dog doesn't like you either."

When Crystal glanced at Mulligan with a speculative look, Logan added, "And if you do anything to hurt Mulligan, I promise you, you'll regret it."

The threat in his voice finally got through to her. Her eyes widened and she took a step back. "I wouldn't do anything to that cute little doggie. I love you."

He snorted. "No, you don't. You just think you do for some reason." He took a step toward her. "And why would that be? Why are you so insistent on pursuing me when it's obvious I'm not interested?"

She cringed and hesitated, something like guilt appearing on her face. Taylor was right—Crystal did have a reason. But she wiped that away with a confident smile. "Don't be silly. We're meant to be together."

Ignoring that obvious lie, Logan said, "No sane person would continue this pursuit without encouragement or some kind of ulterior motive. I'm engaged, remember?"

"Ha," Crystal exclaimed as if she'd caught him in a lie. "Then why haven't you set a wedding date yet?"

"We have," Logan lied, to get that idea out of her head. "We're just waiting to announce it at the engagement party." At her speculative expression, he added, "Which you are *not* invited to." He moved to the driver's side of his car and put Mulligan inside. "If you persist in this idiocy, I'll get a restraining order against you. Violate that, and you'll land in jail."

"But—"

Sick of her, Logan snapped, "Don't you get it? I don't love you. I don't even like you. I love Taylor. I always have."

With that, he got in and slammed the door, peeling out of there while she stood with her mouth agape.

"I love Taylor. I always have." Yeah, he'd said that to get rid of his annoying stalker, but it had a ring of truth to it. *Whoa.* Could it be...?

❧ ❧ ❧ ❧

THE NEXT MORNING AT BREAKFAST, Ryan gave Logan a questioning look, so he was careful not to get too close to Taylor after her father left for work. Once Coach was gone, he told Ryan and Taylor about his run-in with Crystal. "The more I think about this, the more I'm convinced she doesn't really want me, but I have no idea why she's so persistent." He glanced at Ryan. "Did you find out anything?"

"Not yet. But I've got some feelers out."

Logan nodded, then gave Taylor an apologetic look. "She said she didn't believe we were engaged because we haven't set a wedding date yet, so I told her we were going to announce it at the engagement party."

Taylor smiled. "No problem. We'll make one up."

"Yeah," Ryan said. "You can make it far away, so we can get rid of her before the date ever comes to pass."

Logan nodded. "Mom has kind of been pushing me for a date, too."

"Sherry suggested this June," Taylor said. "I told her that was too soon, but she seemed to think next June was too far away."

"Split the difference?" Logan suggested. "Say...around Christmas or New Year's? Or maybe Valentine's Day?"

"Valentine's Day isn't good," Taylor said, "since there's a big dance coming up then, but December should be good, though probably not Christmas day."

"What does it matter?" Ryan asked. "It's not like it's really going to happen."

Color rose in Taylor's cheeks. "I know. I just meant people wouldn't believe it if we set it on those days."

"She's right," Logan said, feeling the need to rescue Taylor. "How about we say the second Saturday in December?"

Taylor pulled up the calendar app on her phone. "Yeah, that should work. It's not so close to Christmas that it would be unbelievable." She grimaced at Logan. "And we can tell your mom we want a Christmas-themed wedding, so she'll be happy that we have a plan for colors and stuff."

"Good," Ryan said. "It's settled then. But I have another suggestion. How about I contact one of the reporters who've been bugging you and set up an exclusive interview? You can tell your story your way, instead of what that gossip website said. Maybe Crystal will finally believe it once it's in print."

Taylor looked uncertain. "You think we can pull that off?"

Logan smiled. "I have no doubt. I'll just let you do most of the talking."

She laughed, as he hoped she would. "Okay. We can discuss things ahead of time so we sound convincing."

"You mean practice?" Logan asked with a grin.

Ryan sent him a quelling glance as Taylor's cheeks turned pink again.

To save her from Ryan's speculation, Logan added, "I told Crystal she wasn't invited to our party, but I don't know if that'll keep her away."

"Well, Hal said he'd throw her out if she showed up at the 19th Hole again," Taylor said.

Ryan raised a finger. "You know, it's odd how she keeps finding you. I know this is a small town, but it's not that small."

"You're right," Logan said slowly.

"You think she's tracking you somehow?" Taylor asked.

"I wouldn't put it past her," Logan said dryly. "She might have put a GPS tracker on my car."

"How would you know?"

Logan thought for a moment. "I always lock my car, so she probably didn't put one inside. But there might be one on the outside of the car. Some are magnetic."

Ryan rose from the table. "And with those tight dresses she wears, she wouldn't be able to lean down or get too far underneath to conceal it too well. I bet we'd be able to find it right away. Let's look."

They all headed out the door and began searching under the vehicle using the flashlight apps on their phones.

"What if we don't find one?" Taylor asked.

Logan got down on his knees to peer under the front bumper. "We can ask a mechanic to jack up the car and take a better look. Plus there's probably a way to find one electronically."

"No need. Here it is," Ryan called. "Right under the wheel well." He held up a small black box, about the size of a pack of cigarettes with a red light on it.

"How do we turn it off?" Taylor asked.

Ryan shrugged. "Unhook the battery, I guess. Or smash the thing into little pieces."

Tempting, but... "I have a better idea," Logan said, taking it from Ryan's hand. "Is Johnson's Ranch Supply still in business?"

"Yes," Taylor said, her brow wrinkled in puzzlement.

"Then I think I'll take a quick trip out there and put this on a ranch vehicle, preferably one heading far out of town."

Taylor grinned. "Great idea. Can you imagine Crystal showing up in a cow pasture looking for you?"

They all laughed. "Now that I'd like to see," Logan said. "Okay, I'll do it," he added with satisfied determination. With these plans in place, he finally felt as if he was getting ahead of the Crystal problem. Now if only he could get rid of her, but still keep Taylor somehow....

CHAPTER ELEVEN

GOOD THING TAYLOR had spent time with Logan at Sanctuary, because she didn't get to see much of him the next few
days, between her working on the wedding invitation job
and him doing physical therapy, plus Ryan taking him off
to do heaven knew what. She suspected Ryan was deliberately trying to keep them apart at times. A throwback from
when they were teenagers...or did he not think they
belonged together? She shrugged. He might not even be
aware he was doing it.

No matter. Today, she'd definitely see a lot of Logan,
since the interview Ryan had arranged with a reporter was
here at home this afternoon, and the engagement party
was tonight. She wasn't really looking forward to the stress
of either event.

Ryan had invited the reporter—someone he said was
fair—to their home, and he was due to arrive any minute.
Taylor checked her appearance in the mirror for the
dozenth time. The simple, short-sleeved lavender wrap
dress hugged her curves, yet looked professional too, so
the guy wouldn't think she was some dumb blonde...like a

particular groupie she could name. She just hoped it conveyed the image of someone who was worthy of golf superstar Logan Kelly.

Time to find out. She went downstairs to join Logan and Ryan, a whole legion of butterflies doing maneuvers in her stomach. The guys were in the living room, chatting, and both looked up as she approached. "Is this okay?" she asked, gesturing down at her dress.

Logan's smile widened. "Perfect," he said, admiration shining in his eyes. "You look beautiful." He looked gorgeous, too, in a navy sports jacket and open-necked white shirt that showed off his tan and sun-lightened brown hair.

"Yeah," Ryan said. "You two will look good for the pictures."

"Pictures?" Taylor repeated. She hadn't known there would be a permanent record of her short engagement.

"Yeah, didn't I say? The reporter is bringing a photographer, too."

That made sense, though it just made her feel more guilty. "Oh, okay. Where do you want me?"

This was Ryan's idea, so he took over. "I figure you two can sit on the couch here, and the reporter, photographer, and I will sit opposite you in the chairs."

Logan's outstretched hand invited her to join him on the couch, so she did. Not wanting to presume too much, she left about a foot in between them.

"No, that won't do," Logan said with a grin. "My fiancée should be closer." He put an arm around her and she scooched over as he gathered her close. Oh my. He smelled so nice, and the warmth of his body pressed up against hers made her want to sink into him.

"That's better," he said with a grin. "You nervous?"

What gave her away? Her tense posture? Her white-knuckled hands clasped together in her lap? "A little," she admitted.

He laid a hand on hers and said, "You look like you're about to face a firing squad instead of spending time with your fiancé. Relax." He gently pried one of her hands loose and held it, interlocking their fingers.

His concern for her was touching, and she relaxed a little.

"There, that's better," he said.

"Yeah," Ryan said. "Now it doesn't look like you're afraid he's going to beat you."

She threw her brother an annoyed glance.

"Ignore him," Logan said with a laugh. "Focus on me." He put one finger on her chin and turned her to face him.

Oh, dear heaven. He was so close, so irresistible, she couldn't help but melt into him. The doorbell rang then, and Ryan went to answer it. "Are you going to answer most of the questions?" she asked Logan softly. "I mean, they're really here because of you, not me."

"If you want me to," Logan said. "I have lots of experience with dealing with the press. But feel free to jump in at any time." He leaned a little closer and murmured, "Now is a good time to put our practice to the test, don't you think?"

Gulping, she couldn't do anything but nod. Anytime he wanted to "practice" was fine with her.

He put both arms around her and kissed her gently, thoroughly, and she couldn't help but respond in kind, reaching up to slip her hand behind his neck. Who cared if it was for show? *You decided to enjoy this, remember?*

Ryan cleared his throat, and Taylor reluctantly pulled away from their kiss, certain her cheeks were flaming red. But at least she was no longer nervous. The kiss had left her feeling calm and centered, yet yearning for more.

Logan stood, and she stood with him while Ryan introduced the reporter and the photographer—the slight, graying reporter's name was Will...something, and she thought the sharp-dressing photographer's name was Leon. She was so flustered by Logan's kiss that they didn't really register.

Logan shook their hands, while not letting go of hers. They sat down where Ryan indicated, and Taylor glanced uncertainly up at Logan. "Oh, you have a little lipstick..."

She grabbed a tissue from the box on the end table and reached up to wipe away the evidence of their kiss. He grinned down at her, and she said lightly, "Might look a little odd for the pictures."

"I wouldn't mind," Logan said softly, gazing into her eyes as if she was the moon and the stars.

She knew it was for the benefit of the reporter, but she didn't care. This felt so wonderful, she didn't want it to end.

"Speaking of pictures," Leon said. "I'll just take a few candid photos while you're talking, and we'll get some more posed ones afterward."

When Logan nodded, Will asked, "Do you mind if I record this as well as take notes?"

"No problem," Logan assured him as he snuggled Taylor close to his side.

"You announced your retirement. Is that final, or do you plan on coming back to golf someday?"

"Oh, it's final," Logan said. "Besides the injury to my shoulder, I'm tired of the nomadic party lifestyle." He gazed down at Taylor. "I want to settle down in one place."

"What's up for you next, then? You're too young to completely retire and do nothing."

"You're right about that," Logan said with a laugh. "I am

working on something, but it's too premature to talk about it right now."

He was? That was news to her. What exactly was he working on? She tried to keep her surprise off her face as Logan gazed down at her. "But one thing I do know—I'm staying here in Dogwood with Taylor."

She couldn't help but beam back at him. Was that the truth...or just a line he was feeding the reporter? She hoped he'd stay and, when this fake engagement was over, maybe she could show him how right they were for each other.

The reporter, who kept an unreadable expression on his face, turned to Taylor. "So, I understand you're a waitress?"

Was that judgment in his tone? She thought he was going to be impartial. "Not anymore," she said, ignoring the implied sneer. "I'm actually starting my own business— a calligraphy business to do wedding stationery, store signs, that sort of thing. One of the first jobs I'll tackle is our wedding." She smiled up at Logan.

"Uh huh," Will said doubtfully, his gaze raking her face. "But I heard this whole thing is a sham, and there isn't really going to be a wedding. Isn't that true?"

Logan squeezed her hand in reassurance, but Taylor didn't need it. The reporter's attack made her steel her spine and forget about nervousness. "No, of course not," she lied. "I can see someone has been feeding you a bunch of nonsense. Let me guess...Crystal?"

Will frowned slightly. Ah hah. She *had* gotten to him. "So it's not a sham?" he asked pointedly.

"No," Logan said and drew Taylor even closer. "Her brother is my best friend," he nodded at Ryan, "and we've known each other since we were kids. There was always something between us, but until we grew up and I moved away, we never acted on it."

"Not until he came home between tournaments," Taylor said. "Then we started dating and..."

"Fell in love," Logan finished for her. He smiled down at her as if he really meant it.

"Why didn't anyone know about this before?" the reporter persisted.

Taylor leapt in to answer. "Logan is so sweet. He knows I don't care for a lot of attention from the press, so he agreed to keep it a secret...for me."

Logan grinned down at her. "Admit it, sweetie. That's not the only reason." She smiled back up at him and shrugged, not knowing where he was going with this. "She didn't want to be a golf widow while I gallivanted all around the country, so she wouldn't agree to marry me until I agreed to give it up and stay here with her in Dogwood."

"No regrets in giving up the game?" Will persisted.

"None at all," Logan assured him. "It's time to settle down. You know, with a wife, a couple of kids, and the whole white picket fence thing."

I wish.

Will still didn't look convinced. "When is the wedding? I hear you haven't set a date yet."

Logan glanced down at Taylor. "Well, *I* wanted to just hop over to Vegas..." Taylor played along, wrinkling her nose at him. "But Taylor and my mom wouldn't hear of it. They want the whole shebang."

Taylor pushed at his chest playfully. "We'll only be married once," she said. "I want to make it memorable."

Logan nodded. "And it would look odd for her new wedding stationery business if she didn't use her own wedding to show off her skills."

Clever of him to think of that.

"Then you do have a date set?" Will asked.

Logan nodded. "Yep, and we plan to announce it tonight at our engagement party."

Taylor patted his chest. "It's okay, honey. You can tell him—the magazine won't come out until afterward."

"I don't remember the actual date, but it's in December," Logan said.

Ryan laughed, sounding relieved that the interview was proceeding okay. "You'd better learn the date quickly, pal. She won't forgive you if you forget your anniversary."

"I'm sending out 'save the date' cards next week," Taylor told him. "So Logan won't forget."

Holding a hand to his chest in mock horror, Logan said, "Who, me?" Dropping the act, he added, "Actually, I didn't forget. I just don't want the actual date in print." He cocked an eyebrow at the reporter. "Just in case some 'fans' decide to invite themselves."

Good save. The reporter nodded, then thankfully got off the subject of their engagement and asked Logan some questions about himself and his golf career. He obviously admired Logan, and even drew Ryan in for a few memories of his time on the tour.

Then, when she thought Will was finally done, he glanced at Taylor once again, then back at Logan. "Word around the tour is that you wouldn't date anyone your dog didn't like. Is that true?"

"True," Logan said with a laugh. Then to Ryan, he said, "Why don't you let Mulligan in?" Returning to the reporter, he added, "For some reason, he doesn't like most women. He certainly doesn't like Crystal. Your source, I assume."

When Ryan opened the door, the little dog ran in and jumped between them on the couch. Taylor scratched his ear with her free hand, and the dog licked it, his tail wagging as he gazed up at her. Thank goodness.

"See?" Logan said in triumph. "He adores Taylor."

"And I adore him," Taylor said truthfully, then laughed as Mulligan turned over to present his belly for rubbing. Grinning, she obliged. He deserved it for corroborating their story.

"I can see that," Will said slowly. "I guess my source fed me some bad intel."

His source? Why be so evasive. It was obvious his source was Crystal.

Logan nodded. "For some reason, she's been stalking me and refuses to believe I'm engaged to Taylor."

"She even put a GPS tracker on his car," Taylor added, shaking her head. "We don't know why she's so persistent, though it is annoying."

Will exchanged a glance with Leon. "I might have some ideas on that."

Thank goodness. It finally looked as though he believed them.

"I'd love to hear them," Logan said fervently.

"Let me check around, and if I learn something, I'll get back to you. Off the record, of course."

"Of course," Logan agreed.

Leon held up his camera. She'd noticed him taking some photos during the interview, but now he said, "Can I get a few posed shots?"

"Sure," Logan said, squeezing her hand. "Where do you want us?"

"In front of the fireplace, I think."

He took some pictures of Logan alone, and some of the two of them. In each one, Logan held on tight to her waist or her hand, and gave her loving looks, making it clear, to the photographer at least, that he was smitten with her.

"One last picture, please," Leon said. "Would you mind kissing her again for the audience?"

"Mind?" Logan said with a grin. "I insist." With that, he grabbed Taylor and dipped her. His eyes crinkled in amusement as he gazed down at her, and she laughed up at him, loving his playful side.

"Me, too," she said, and reached up to cup his head in her hand.

He kissed her slowly, passionately, as the camera clicked away. She returned his kiss with equal fervor, wishing they could be like this for the rest of their lives.

When Ryan cleared his throat again, Logan finally let up on the kiss. "Save it for the honeymoon," Ryan said gruffly.

Feeling flushed and flustered, Taylor patted her hair back into place.

"Yep, my source was definitely wrong," Will said, then shook their hands.

"Would it be possible to get copies of some of those photos?" Taylor asked Leon. It would be nice to have something to remember their time together.

"Sure," he said. "I'll email them to Ryan."

After he and Leon left, Taylor collapsed back onto the couch, giving Mulligan another belly rub for good behavior.

"That went well, I think," Logan said.

Taylor nodded. "So long as he tells the truth, we're good."

Ryan cocked his head. "You mean, so long as he tells the story the way we want him to."

"Of course," Taylor said quickly. Thank goodness Logan was paying more attention to Mulligan right now and didn't see her flushed cheeks.

As Ryan babbled to Logan about how great the interview went, Taylor sighed in relief. Now she only had to get through the engagement party tonight.

❖ ❖ ❖ ❖

FOR THE PARTY, she changed into a little black dress she had purchased especially for this occasion. Short, with spaghetti straps and a form-fitting shape with a small slit above the knee, it was more daring than anything she'd ever worn before, but she needed something to boost her confidence for the night.

She went downstairs to meet Logan, Ryan, and her father. They all looked handsome in their suits, and she wondered if her dress was too much. But when she saw Logan's jaw-dropped reaction, her confidence surged. Yes, the dress was a good choice.

He grabbed her hands and took a step back, looking her up and down. "Wow. I've never seen you look like this."

Her father nodded. "You look great, honey."

Ryan scowled. "Won't you get cold in that?"

"I have a wrap for when I'm outside," she told him, gesturing with the lacy shawl she had folded over her arm.

Logan was the perfect attentive fiancé as he placed the shawl around her shoulders. "Don't worry," he murmured. "I'll keep you warm."

Her heart leapt with excitement. Maybe he'd just said it for her father's benefit, but she couldn't help but feel joy anyway. Maybe tonight wouldn't be so bad after all.

"What's the plan?" Ryan asked. "Will there be drinks?"

She shrugged. "I don't know. Ask Dad. He and Sherry planned the whole thing. All I did was give them a guest list. They said I wouldn't have to do anything, so I didn't."

Her father snorted. "Well, I didn't have much to do with it—it was mostly Sherry. I think you'll like what she came up with." He checked his watch. "She wants you two to arrive a little after the other guests, so I think it's safe to go now."

Taylor's stomach was a ball of nerves as Logan drove to the 19th Hole at the golf course. Would everyone see through their ruse? Would she give it away somehow? She didn't think she could bear it if she did.

Her father rode with Ryan, and once they arrived and exited the cars, her father motioned to Ryan. "Let's go in first, let Sherry know they're here." He glanced back at Logan. "Oh, and you don't have to worry about Crystal showing up. Taylor's bartender friend Adam offered to act as bouncer to keep the riffraff out."

Well, that was a relief. As her father and brother entered the building, Taylor stood alone with Logan out in the cool night air under the portico. "Nervous?" he asked.

"Is it so obvious?" she asked ruefully.

"Probably only to me," he assured her. "But you have nothing to worry about. You look stunning, and every man there will envy me."

She doubted it, but she appreciated him trying to put her at ease.

He rubbed her arm, adding, "Just relax and enjoy the evening. I know I'm going to."

She took a deep breath. "Okay. I can do that." She'd enjoy being with Logan, no matter where they were.

"I think we've delayed long enough," Logan said, and offered her his arm. "Shall we go in, milady?"

Smiling, Taylor took his arm. "Why yes, kind sir. I do believe we shall."

When they entered the foyer of the bar/restaurant, Taylor peeked inside. She barely recognized it. White tulle and fairy lights draped the walls and columns to disguise and soften the masculine appearance of the place, and white tablecloths with fragrant white flowers and candles made it even more like a fairyland.

Sherry came forward to greet them, hugging her son.

"This is absolutely gorgeous," Taylor gushed. "I can't believe you made this place look so...so...bridal." For lack of a better word.

"Thanks, Mom," Logan added. "You have no idea how much we appreciate this."

"You're welcome," Sherry said, hugging Taylor. "It was the least I could do for my only son and my future daughter-in-law." She patted Logan on the arm. "I'll get you both a glass of champagne. Stay here, and we'll make the announcement in a few minutes."

Adam stood by the door inside the foyer, looking darkly handsome in a suit and tie. Logan clapped him on the back and shook his hand. "Thanks, man. We really do appreciate this."

"No problem," Adam said. "I'll make sure there are no party crashers."

Taylor hugged him. "You're the best." With Adam on the job, she no longer worried about Crystal showing up to make a mockery of their party. Sherry had done such a great job, she didn't want to ruin it for her.

Sherry pushed her way through the crowd toward them, two glasses of bubbly in her hands. "Champagne?" she offered.

Taylor didn't really drink much, but it would probably make her relax a little. Besides, it was probably expected of her. "Thank you," she said as they both took a glass.

"Come with me," Sherry said. "Your father is about to make the announcement."

She led them toward a small portable stage, where her father stood holding a microphone close to his mouth. "Hello?" he said tentatively. The sound system squealed and everyone stopped talking to look at him. He reared away from the mic. "Well, that's not exactly how I wanted to get your attention, but whatever works."

They all laughed, and her father continued. "Does everyone have a glass?" A rustle passed through the crowd as everyone picked up a glass of something, whether champagne, punch, or whatever.

When the rustling subsided, her father motioned to Logan and Taylor. "Come on up here."

They stepped up onto the stage, Taylor feeling self-conscious with all the eyes staring at her. Logan slid his arm around her waist, holding her steady.

Her father continued, "For those of you who don't know me, I'm Tommy Nash, Taylor's father. Logan's mother, Sherry, and I are happy and proud to announce the engagement of our children, Taylor and Logan." He raised his glass. "To the happy couple."

The people in the crowd repeated his words, and Taylor looked up at Logan. He leaned down to kiss her. Though she was nervous in front of all these people, she forgot all that when his lips met hers. The crowd cheered and applauded, and they all seemed so happy about the engagement, Taylor blinked back tears as she took a sip of her champagne.

"Thank you, everyone," her father said. "Now, here's Sherry, the mastermind of this shindig, to tell you about what's going on tonight."

Sherry took the mic from him, looking comfortable being the center of attention. Taylor never would've guessed that. "Thank you, everyone, for coming tonight and celebrating the engagement of these two wonderful people. I know you want to see them kiss often..." The crowd chuckled. "But banging silverware on glasses can be annoying, so tonight, if you want to see them kiss, you have to sing them at least one verse of a love song."

Gauging by the approval of the crowd, it sounded like there would be a lot of kissing going on tonight. Taylor glanced up at Logan to see if he was okay with it, but he just grinned down at her. Could it be that he enjoyed it as much as she did?

"Also," Sherry added, "in the vein of our recently discovered town time capsule, I asked each of you to bring something small to put in a special time capsule to remind the happy couple of tonight, to be opened on their tenth anniversary."

Taylor kept her smile firmly in place, though her heart sank at the knowledge there wouldn't even be a first anniversary.

Sherry continued, "That's in the back on the left. We've also set up a selfie photo booth in the back on the right with props, plus a video camera so you can record any advice you might have for a newly married couple."

"When's the wedding?" someone called from the back of the room.

Sherry turned to Logan and Taylor with a questioning look, offering them the mic.

Taylor shook her head vehemently, but Logan took it with confidence. "Taylor will be sending out 'save the date' cards soon, but I guess it wouldn't hurt to let you know that we've selected the second Saturday in December to tie the knot. We hope to see you all there."

Sherry beamed at them and took the mic back. "So, there you have it. Please, enjoy yourselves."

Wow—Sherry really had put a lot of thought into this. Though Taylor felt like shrinking away, she couldn't disappoint Sherry or her friends. They surged forward now, to offer their congratulations.

"I'm so happy for you," Amber said, giving her a hug.

Lauren, Julie, and Annie weren't far behind. Taylor blinked back tears once more. She had such wonderful friends.

Amber glanced around mischievously. "Ready, girls?"

They nodded, and launched into a rousing, if slightly off-tune, rendition of John Legend's *All of Me.* Part of it, anyway.

Taylor laughed and clapped, appreciating their enthusiasm, if not their singing.

"Well?" Amber asked, looking significantly at Logan.

"That definitely deserves a kiss, don't you think?" he asked Taylor. "I do love 'all your curves and all your edges.'" He waggled his eyebrows at her.

Taylor laughed, happy that Logan was playing along so well. "Yes, I think so," she said.

Logan dipped her into another kiss, and Taylor leaned into it, putting on a show for her friends. When Taylor came up for air, breathless, they laughed and applauded.

"Does this mean we get to be your bridesmaids?" Amber asked.

"Of course," Taylor assured them. "Who else would I ask?" It made them so elated, she couldn't even feel bad about deceiving them. Let them feel happy for awhile.

"Our turn," one of her father's cronies said, pushing his way forward. He and his wife sang a remarkably good version of *Love Will Keep Us Together.* Something they'd obviously done before.

Taylor quirked an eyebrow at Logan, and he swooped in to kiss her, thankfully not dipping her again—that was a bit dizzying.

The rest of the evening went much like that, with Logan hugging her to his side and kissing her every time someone sang a verse. She didn't know why she'd been so nervous—she was having a great time, the champagne and Logan's enthusiastic kisses making her feel a bit heady.

After a while, though, she excused herself to use the ladies' room, and when she came out, Ryan was there. He pulled her aside, and said softly, "You look like you're enjoying yourself."

"I am. Dad and Sherry did a great job putting this party together."

He nodded. "They did, but...you look like you're enjoying yourself a bit too much."

She gave him a startled look. "Isn't that what I'm supposed to do?"

"For appearances, yes. But..."

"But what?" she asked in trepidation.

"I know you had a crush on him before, and I thought you got over that. But you didn't, did you? You love him."

She should have known Ryan would figure it out. She smiled ruefully. No sense in denying it. "Yes, I do. I always have." She grabbed his arm. "You're not going to tell him, are you?"

Ryan gave her a pitying look. "No, but...you know he doesn't feel the same, right? This is all just an act, and it will end someday. As soon as Crystal is gone."

Taylor's eyes filled with tears. She nodded. "I know."

He hugged her with one arm. "I just don't want to see you so far gone that you're devastated when all this comes to an end."

She gave him a tremulous smile. "Too late."

"If you want me to tell him to cool it, I will."

She shook her head. "No. I—I'm fine." Giving him a rueful shrug, she added, "I want to enjoy it while it lasts."

"Okay," Ryan said. "I just don't want you to be hurt."

"I know," she acknowledged, but couldn't thank him for his concern. Not when he'd just burst her bright, happy bubble. "Promise me you won't tell him."

He gave her a hug. "Yes, I promise. He won't hear it from me."

She glanced around for Logan. He was shaking hands

with Hal, the owner of this place, both of them looking satisfied. "Can you, uh, tell Logan I'm not feeling well and want to go home? And make my apologies to everyone?" It wasn't a lie. She covered her stomach with one hand, afraid she was going to throw up. "It's the champagne, I think."

"Of course," Ryan said with sympathy.

As he left to get Logan, she resisted the urge to cry. Oh, she knew in the back of her mind that this fairytale would all end someday soon, but why did Ryan have to remind her *now?*

CHAPTER TWELVE

THE NEXT MORNING, Taylor came downstairs to cook breakfast, only to find that Logan had already started it. Ryan and her father sat at the kitchen table, their plates already full. "What's this?" she asked in surprise.

Logan grinned at her. "You weren't feeling well last night, so I thought I'd help you out this morning. Besides, since I'm mooching off you guys and getting free room and board, it's the least I can do."

Remembering exactly why she'd felt unwell, Taylor gave him a half smile and poured herself a glass of juice. Feeling she needed to say something, she added, "I didn't know you could cook."

He winked at her. "I aim to be a full-service fiancé."

Her father beamed, looking up from his half-eaten breakfast. "He's making omelets. Let him know what you want in yours."

Why did he have to be so adorable? Hardening her heart, she shrugged. "Whatever you're having." She really wasn't in the mood to eat much anyway.

Ryan gave her a sympathetic look and squeezed her hand. She ignored him—after all, he was the one who'd popped her bubble of happiness and reminded her it wouldn't last.

With his back to her, Logan seemed oblivious to the byplay. "What do you want to do today, Taylor? You finished that job, didn't you?"

"Yes, but I need to get the invitations to Lana." Besides, she wasn't sure she could be around him now, not without remembering how soon it would probably all be over. She was too afraid she'd burst into tears if anyone mentioned the stupid engagement again—the engagement that should never have happened.

"Can't that wait?" Logan asked.

"Probably not," Ryan said, backing her up. "You did tell the reporter you were sending them out soon."

As their father excused himself to go to work, Logan slid a perfectly cooked omelet onto her plate. "There you go." He brought his own plate to join them.

She picked listlessly at her food.

"Are you okay?" Logan asked, looking concerned.

"I'm fine. My stomach is just feeling a little queasy this morning."

Ryan laughed, though it sounded forced to her. "Must have been all that champagne she had last night. Taylor's a lightweight when it comes to alcohol," he confided to Logan.

Obviously, her brother thought he was helping. Not so much.

"Maybe the omelet wasn't such a good idea," Logan said. "Want some toast instead?"

"Uh, sure."

As Logan got up to make toast for her, she kicked her brother under the table.

"Ow," he muttered, rubbing his shin. "I'm just trying to help."

"Well, stop it," she whispered back. Louder, she said, "On second thought, I'll just grab something on the way. I don't want to be late."

Logan looked puzzled, but Ryan distracted him with some inanity as she slipped out of the house.

Not quite feeling herself, she headed to Great Expectations Event Planning. Though she didn't really have an exact time to meet Lana, she'd promised to get the invitations to her sometime today. She placed the neatly boxed job on Lana's desk.

Lana opened one to take a look and smiled. "You always do such great work. Are you ready for more jobs?"

"Well, I have the place cards, signs, and seating chart to do as well..."

"We won't need those until right before the wedding."

Taylor nodded. "I also need to do my own 'save the date' cards, but I can do some other jobs, sure." After all, that's what this fake engagement was all about—giving her a chance to make her own small business work. And keeping busy would keep her mind off Logan.

Lana brightened. "Oh, you've set a date?"

Feeling like a fraud, Taylor told her what they'd decided on.

"Awesome. Can Great Expectations help you with the planning?" Lana asked with an expectant grin.

Taylor should have known this question was coming. "I hadn't thought that far ahead," she admitted. Trying to buy some time, she added, "Of course, I'd love that. But Logan's mom wants to help, so I need to talk to her first. We'll set up an appointment to see you later."

"Perfect. So, talking about other jobs, I do have another wedding coming up soon, but don't have the details nailed down yet. However, someone heard about what you do and called me to get your contact information. I didn't want to give it out without your permission, but I told her I was seeing you today and would ask you to call her."

Someone she didn't know had heard of her and was interested in using her services? She should be delighted, but her stupid mood was killing what should be elation.

"Great," she said. "I'll call her."

Lana gave her the information, paid her for her work on the invitations, then walked Taylor to the door. "Remember, give me a call when you and Logan's mom want to meet. I'd love to help you out."

"Will do," Taylor said with a smile. After she sat in her Mini Cooper, she glanced at the piece of paper Lana had given her. Makayla Smith. Might as well give her a call and set something up.

She dialed and heard a breathless, "Hello?" on the other end.

"Makayla Smith?"

"Uh, yes, that's me."

"This is Taylor Nash. Lana from Great Expectations said you wanted to talk to me about doing a potential calligraphy job for you?"

"Oh, yes. Yes, I do. Can we meet? Today, some time?"

Surprised by the short notice, Taylor said, "Uh, sure."

"Can you meet now for coffee?"

"Now?"

"Yes, I'm visiting a friend here in Dogwood, and I'm leaving in a couple of days, so I'd like to get started as soon as possible."

Taylor didn't have any pressing appointments, so she said, "Okay, I can do that."

"Good. I'm not really familiar with the town, so where do you suggest?"

"How about the Blossom Café?" When Makayla agreed, Taylor gave her directions and hung up. Well, at least something good would come out of this fake engagement.

She drove to the café and got a booth, then realized she didn't know what the woman looked like. She thought about calling her back, but then saw a brunette walk in the door. Young, with designer jeans, skyscraper heels, a humongous purse hooked over her arm, and enough bling to make the Kardashians jealous, she obviously didn't live here in Dogwood. Taylor's hopes rose. It definitely looked as though the woman could afford to pay her rates. She raised her hand, and the woman minced over, not able to go very fast in those ridiculous heels. Everyone's gaze followed her.

"Ms. Smith?" Taylor asked.

"Oh, call me Makayla," the woman said, and sat down. "I assume you're Taylor Nash?"

"Yes."

She peered around the restaurant, decorated in pink and black with dogwood blossoms painted on the walls. "Isn't this...quaint?"

Taylor resisted the urge to defend the restaurant. She didn't really care what the client thought about the surroundings—selling her services was more important now. Luckily, Tina came over then to wait on them. "Tea and cinnamon roll?" she asked Taylor.

Taylor nodded, smiling. "You do know what I like."

Makayla didn't even look at the menu. "I'd like a nonfat, half caff, sugar-free caramel macchiato with sprinkles—make sure it's not too hot, and put it in the largest mug you have."

Tina lowered her ticket book and raised her eyebrows. "Do I look like a barista?" When Makayla stared blankly back at her, Tina said flatly, "We have coffee." Her tone said "take it or leave it."

Makayla pouted and waved her hand dismissively. "Just water."

Entitled much? Taylor hoped the woman wouldn't be too much of a pain to work with. As Tina walked away, Makayla placed her enormous bag on the bench seat beside her.

"Lana said you were looking for a calligrapher?" Taylor asked.

"Oh, yes," Makayla gushed. "I heard about you from my friend. She loves your work, so I thought I'd see if you can help me."

"What do you need done?" Taylor smiled up at Tina as she left Taylor's order, rolled her eyes, and left.

"Well, I'm getting married," Makayla said, and squealed. "It's so exciting. I'll need all the wedding stuff done."

"Wedding stuff? The stationery, you mean?"

"Yes, invitations, all of that." She waved her hand dismissively again. "I'm sure you know better than I do."

Okaaay... Taylor pulled out a rate card she'd made up last week. "This is how much I charge for various wedding stationery needs. I can give you a better idea of the cost if you let me know how many guests you'll have. And when is your wedding? How much time do we have to get everything done?" She took a bite of her cinnamon roll, wondering if she even wanted to work for this woman. Then again, she had to take as many jobs as she could to get the business started.

Makayla glanced at the rate card, then stuck in in her purse. Did she even read it? "This is fine. I'll get you the other information later." Then, changing the subject, she said, "You've lived in Dogwood for a long time, right?"

"All my life."

"Want to hear some gossip?"

Taylor opened her mouth to say "Not really," but Makayla didn't wait for her answer. "You must know Logan Kelly, the famous golfer, right?"

"I do." What was this all about?

Makayla glanced around as if she wanted to make sure no one overheard them—a surefire way to ensure everyone swiveled their ears in their direction. "Well, I heard he's engaged to some waitress, but I saw him with someone else a little while ago. Do you believe it? He's cheating on the little waitress."

The cinnamon roll felt like lead in her stomach. "Oh?" she said, noncommittally, not wanting to admit that she was that "little waitress."

"Yes—a gorgeous blonde in a tight dress."

Crystal? Really? Her heart sank. Had he finally given in?

"He had her plastered up against his car and was kissing her like he hadn't had a woman in years. And his hands weren't exactly PG either, if you know what I mean." Makayla fanned herself with her hand. "Hot, hot, hot. If my fiancé kissed someone else like that, I'd leave him so fast, he'd have skid marks on his body."

She wasn't keeping her voice down, and several gasps came from around them.

Wait. That didn't sound like Logan at all. And Makayla's eyes flashed with what looked like malicious glee.

Anger filled Taylor. "I don't believe you," she said, loud enough so everyone who wanted to could hear. "Logan has too much class, too much honor, to do anything like that." It didn't matter that their engagement was fake, he would never do that. He would never disrespect her.

Annoyed, Makayla spat back, "You didn't see what I saw."

"You made that up," Taylor accused her. "You obviously know who I am, and that I'm Logan's fiancée."

Makayla widened her eyes, and put a hand over her mouth in mock horror. "I'm so sorry," she said. *Insincere much?* "I didn't know—"

"Save it for someone who cares," Taylor bit off. "You're lying. Crystal put you up to this, right? What are you trying to pull?" She should have known—the two looked like they came from the same mold.

Before the woman could utter another falsehood, Taylor leaned in and stabbed her finger toward Makayla's chest. "If you ever repeat that, or any other lies about Logan, you'll not only have a slander lawsuit on your hands, but you'll have me to reckon with. Got that?"

Applause filled the diner, and someone from the back yelled, "Go, Taylor. You tell her!"

Makayla obviously realized she was defeated, because she grabbed her bag and stood, slamming it under her arm with a vicious expression. "You and this stupid town are nothing but a bunch of inbred hicks. Logan is meant to be with Crystal, not a stupid little waitress who doesn't even know how to dress herself."

That was the worst insult she could come up with? Amusement abated some of the anger, especially when Taylor realized the restaurant's patrons were on her side.

Makayla wrenched the rate card out of her purse and tore it in half, throwing the pieces at Taylor. "And your business is a joke."

"No, honey, you're the joke," Tina drawled behind her.

Makayla put her nose in the air, and tried to stomp out of the diner, but couldn't quite do it in those stupid shoes. She settled for sort of scooting out in mincing little steps as fast as she could go.

Tina patted her on the shoulder. "Thanks for the entertainment. Your meal is on me."

"Thank you," Taylor said in a small voice. Though Crystal's friend had gone, anger still pumped through her. But now it was tinged with a bit of dread. Would the stupid woman repeat her lies to anyone else? Would Logan constantly be tied with Crystal in the public's eye?

Not if Taylor had anything to do with it. This had to stop.

CHAPTER THIRTEEN

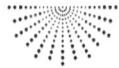

As Logan waited for Ryan to meet him for lunch at The Spot, he had some time to think about what had happened over the past few days. What was up with Taylor? She'd been so fun, so open, so very kissable at the engagement party, then shut down at the end of it. He didn't buy her excuse of not feeling well anymore. Not after she wouldn't even meet his eyes this morning at breakfast.

Had he offended her somehow? He thought back over the night. If he had, he sure didn't know how.

Ryan joined him then, and before Ryan could say anything, Logan asked, "Do you know what's wrong with Taylor?"

"Well, hello to you, too," Ryan said with sarcasm. "I'm fine, how are you?"

"Come on," Logan said in annoyance. "We've known each other long enough not to need small talk."

"Yeah, but you don't usually launch into interrogation mode the moment you see me."

"Interrogation mode? I asked one question." Logan

narrowed his eyes at Ryan. "You do know what's wrong. Tell me."

"I—"

Before Ryan could say anything, the restaurant owner, Gina Hayes, came to their table and set down menus. He'd known her and this place forever, it seemed, though this was the first time he'd eaten here since he got back. So, when she lingered to talk, he had to be polite, though he wanted to wring the truth out of Ryan.

She patted them both on their shoulders. "So good to see you two back in town."

"Glad to be back," Logan told her.

"Yeah, we all know why." She grinned at him. "You chose wisely in Taylor. It's always good when your fiancée knows you well enough to know you wouldn't jeopardize the good thing you two have going."

He nodded, though he gave her a quizzical look. What was she talking about? He turned to Ryan who shrugged in response.

"Do you know something we don't?" Ryan asked.

Gina looked surprised. "You haven't heard? Some idiot woman tried to make Taylor believe Logan was cheating on her."

"I would never..." Logan protested. Was that why Taylor was so squirrely?

"I know," Gina said with a smile. "And so did Taylor. She got all fired up and defended you like an avenging goddess. I hear it was quite the scene."

"When was this? Last night?" If so, it might explain her mood.

"No, this morning, at the Blossom."

"What happened, exactly?" Logan asked.

After Gina finished telling him everything she'd heard, an unaccustomed warmth spread through Logan. Any other woman would have believed the lies, would have confronted him immediately with righteous anger. And he wouldn't have blamed her—even though their relationship was a sham, she knew he wouldn't be so disrespectful as to play around on a woman he'd claimed as his fiancée.

But Taylor...Taylor's first thought had been to trust him, to defend him. Wow. She would make a great wife. Unfortunately, this engagement was a lie. She deserved so much more—not a fake fiancé, but a real one. She deserved a genuine relationship, an honest proposal, and a lifetime of happiness with someone. At what point would she have enough of their playacting? When would she tell him to take a hike and open her heart to someone who would give her everything she deserved?

The thought was disturbing and a strange possessiveness filled him at the thought of her being with anyone else.

His self-revelations were interrupted by Ryan, saying, "Thanks for letting us know, Gina."

As Gina left with their drink orders, Logan's thoughts were in a whirl. After this morning, he wasn't sure Taylor even liked him, and yet she'd defended him immediately. "What's going on with her?" he asked Ryan.

"Gina?"

"No, Taylor, you idiot. Why are you being so dense? Stop stalling and tell me what you know."

Ryan sighed. "There's nothing wrong with Taylor. I think it's just that last night was a bit too much for her."

"That's why she was so distant this morning?"

Ryan shrugged. "Probably. Or maybe she's just trying to get some distance from you. You were kind of touchy-feely last night."

Well, yeah, but she seemed to be into it as much as he

was. "It was our engagement party," he snapped. "What was I supposed to do? Keep her at arm's length?"

"No, but dude, you were all over her."

"Since when do you care?"

"Since she's my *sister,*" Ryan bit out. "That's not what she signed up for when she agreed to this plan, and I don't want to see her hurt."

Well, that was a slap in the face, Ryan sounded ticked. Had Taylor said something to him? Logan did vaguely recall them talking together, right before Taylor said she wasn't feeling well and asked to leave.

Gina arrived then to take their orders, and when she was gone, Logan said, "I would never hurt her. You know that."

"Then stop acting like you're in love with her," Ryan snapped.

Whoa. Was he serious? Logan gaped for a moment. "You do know that's what this whole plan was all about, don't you? That's how I'm supposed to act."

"Yes, but..." Ryan's gaze shifted away from him and lowered his voice, "...I don't want Taylor to think it's real."

Ryan was his best friend. He couldn't keep this from him. He had to man up. "What if it is real?" he asked softly.

"What?" The shock on Ryan's face was almost comical.

"If I have fallen in love with Taylor, would that be okay with you?" Logan swallowed hard. He didn't know what he would do if his best friend said no.

"I— I—" Ryan shook his head. *"Are* you? In love with her?"

Logan took a deep breath. He probably should tell Taylor first, but he needed Ryan's approval. "Yes. I am." Logan gave him a half smile, hoping Ryan wouldn't see this as a betrayal.

"Since when?" Ryan demanded, looking shocked and

indignant.

Logan shrugged. "I think I have been most of my life, but I never acted on it because you've always been so protective of her. I didn't want to do anything to spoil our friendship."

Ryan gaped at him. "And now?"

"I just realized a few days ago how much I care about her." No, he owed Ryan the truth. "How much I love her." He gave Ryan a wary glance. "Is that going to be a problem for you?"

Ryan scrubbed his face with both hands as if he couldn't quite believe what was happening. He opened his mouth a couple of times as if he was going to say something, then shut it with a shake of his head. Finally, he said, "It's okay with me if it's okay with Taylor. I just want her to be happy."

"Me, too," Logan said.

"Then you gotta tell her."

"I'm not sure how she'll react." Especially since he kept getting mixed signals from her. He'd thought she was starting to get to know him, to enjoy being around him. But after this morning, he wasn't sure. It was too soon to tell her how he felt. Maybe later, after she got to know him better, and he was sure he wouldn't make a fool of himself by declaring his real love for her.

Ryan muttered something he didn't catch, then held up his hands. "Look, I'm clearly clueless about what's going on with you and my sister. I don't want to get in the middle of this. Just...do your thing and keep me out of it."

"Do you think she—"

"Nope." Ryan shook his head. "Not gonna talk about this anymore. Figure your own mess out."

Gina delivered their order, saying, "Oh, by the way, Logan, you owe someone an apology."

"Sorry, did I do something wrong?"

"Not to me—to Lacy Morgan."

"Why?" He didn't recall ever meeting the woman.

"She's the owner of Second Chance Ranch. It seems some young woman showed up, wearing very little clothes, looking for you."

"Oh. That." The light dawned. Ryan looked puzzled, so Logan explained, "Crystal's tracker."

Ryan grinned. "So that's where it ended up. What did she do?"

"The way I understand it, she barged into the barn looking for you and came face to face with a calf. She screamed, tripped, and landed in a cow patty, ruining her pretty dress." Gina shrugged, her eyes twinkling. "The hired hands were more than happy to help her up, but the dogs chased her off. Lacy was annoyed that she upset the calf."

Logan chuckled, picturing it. "I'll take care of it," he said. "I'll send her flowers...and a bucket of apples for the calf."

"You do that," Gina said, and left them to their lunch.

Ryan shook his head in amusement. "I wish I could have seen that," he said, then snapped his fingers. "Oh, I meant to tell you—I heard back from that reporter."

"Yeah?" Logan asked in trepidation.

Ryan scrolled through his phone and showed him the article with Will's byline on a reputable golf website. "It's a good one. Mostly focuses on you and your retirement. Doesn't say anything about a fake engagement, though it does mention Taylor."

Logan took his word for it and just skimmed the article. They'd used the picture where he dipped Taylor in front of the fireplace. She looked so happy and carefree. He wanted to make her feel that way all the time—for real.

Swallowing a bite of his burger, Ryan added, "He also found out some things about Crystal."

"Such as...?"

"Such as why she's been such a pest." Ryan grinned. "Now I know how to get rid of her. For good, this time."

"Great," Logan said. "Let's hear it."

Ryan regarded him thoughtfully. "I think Taylor needs to be in on this, too. Think you can find out where Crystal's staying?"

"The way this town gossips, I don't think it'll take any time at all."

"Good," Ryan said. "You do that, and I'll talk to Taylor and see if she wants to come along, then we'll end this nonsense."

❖ ❖ ❖ ❖

IT TOOK EVEN LESS time than Logan had thought to track Crystal down. One phone call to the Harrington, and he learned that Crystal was staying there along with her friend Makayla—the one who had tried to spread lies about him. Irene Harrington confided that they were always there in the late afternoon, to get gussied up, as she put it, before they went out on the town and spread more rumors.

He waited with Ryan in the living room as Taylor came downstairs, looking determined and loaded for bear. "You ready to do this?" he asked her.

"Yes," she said with a firm nod. "Let's get this over with."

They all rode over in Logan's car, though Ryan refused to tell them what he had learned. For some reason, he wanted to keep it a secret until they confronted Crystal.

Irene had given them Crystal's room number, and loitered in the hallway, pretending to vacuum, obviously wanting to know what was going to happen. "We don't want any violence here," she told Logan.

"Don't worry," he assured her. "There won't be any of that...unless Crystal attacks us first."

"*I'm* not making any promises," Taylor muttered.

Go, tiger, Logan thought proudly, and slipped an arm around her waist so they could be a united front. "Will you protect me from her?" he asked with a smile.

She gave him the onceover. "Oh, I think you're big enough to take care of yourself."

Ignoring the byplay, Ryan knocked on the door, and Crystal answered it promptly, thankfully already dressed. "What do you want?" she asked, scowling, then changed her tune when she saw Logan. "Oh! I'm so glad you came." Her gaze narrowed at Taylor. "Why'd you bring *her?*"

"We all want to talk to you," Logan said, realizing she'd ignore anyone else. "Can we come in?" Ryan didn't give her a chance to say no as he pushed inside the small room, which was covered in discarded clothes, used plates, and scattered bottles of make-up and other toiletries. Logan closed the door behind them.

She backed up, her gaze darting around the room as if she was a little embarrassed by her mess. Good—maybe they could keep her off guard.

Ryan leapt right in. "I learned something today," he said, smiling wolfishly as he moved forward and backed her against the bed.

The back of her knees hit the mattress, and she sat down abruptly. "What?" She glanced at Taylor with a sneer. "The little waitress hear something she didn't like?"

"The *little waitress,*" Taylor bit out, "wasn't stupid enough to fall for your friend's lies."

Logan grinned and tightened his hold on Taylor, just to

see Crystal scowl. "You used Makayla, really? I'd say nice try, but I'd be lying."

Crystal folded her arms, trying to look as though she was in control, though the three of them had moved close enough to keep her trapped on the bed as they glared down at her.

"No," Ryan said, "I'm talking about a certain club, an agreement some of you groupies have to snare the golfers on the tour."

Crystal looked surprised for a moment. *Bingo.* She lifted her chin. "I don't know what you're talking about."

"What kind of agreement?" Logan asked.

"Well, it seems that Crystal and her friends have a bet going on to see who can score the most points this season."

"Points?" Taylor sounded as confused as Logan felt.

Ryan nodded. "They've assigned numbers to each golfer on the tour, depending on how hard to get they are." Their puzzled expressions urged him to continue, so he added, "They earn points when they have a picture showing up in the tabloids with the guy—the more intimate, the better."

"You have got to be kidding me," Taylor muttered.

"Nope. And Studley Do-Right here is worth a heck of a lot of points. Isn't he, Crystal?"

She pressed her lips together and refused to answer, turning her head away.

But Ryan pressed on. "It seems Crystal is falling behind, so she was hoping to bag Logan and bring her standing to the top."

"Points?" Logan said, not believing what he was hearing. "You've been stalking me and acting like a total idiot for *points?*"

"Well, in her defense, I hear the woman with the highest points at the end of the season wins a huge pot of money."

"Can I hit her now?" Taylor asked, moving forward

menacingly.

Logan grinned and pulled her back. "Naw. She's not worth it."

"Where'd you hear that?" Crystal demanded.

"It's not important," Ryan said. "What is important is that we know. So, give up your stupid pursuit and leave town."

She glanced up at Logan, obviously thinking. "Well, now that you know, all you have to do is lie down with me on this bed, let your caddy take a picture, and I'll be out of here right away." She patted the mattress invitingly.

Logan snorted. "Not gonna happen. Ever."

"What's more," Ryan added, "if you keep this up, I'll let the media know about your club and your game. Think you'll get any of the golfers to give you the time of day after that?"

Livid, Crystal stood up and got right in Ryan's face before she spat out, "That's blackmail."

Before Logan could do anything, Taylor took a step forward and shoved Crystal back on the bed. When Crystal lost her balance and fell on her back, Taylor leaned in and got in *her* face. "You'd better believe it is."

Logan chortled. "Now that's a picture worth some points!"

Taylor slanted a grim glance at him, then turned back to Crystal. "You'd better be out of here by morning, and if you ever show your face in town again, or *ever* tell any more stupid lies about Logan, I'll personally see to it that the whole world knows about your stupid club. You got that?"

Crystal glared at her for a moment, then said, "If you all promise not to tell anyone about the club, I'll leave tomorrow."

"We promise," Logan said as Taylor backed up.

Crystal sat up, looking extremely annoyed. "Now get out of my room or I'll call the cops."

"Gladly," Taylor said, and stalked out, Logan and Ryan right behind her.

When she snatched open the door, Irene almost fell in. Logan grinned—she must have had her ear to the door, and she didn't even look embarrassed about it.

"Good for you," the woman said. "But are you really going to let her get away with that...that point thing?"

Ryan glanced at Logan. "Well, *we* promised not to tell anyone..."

In case she didn't get it, Logan added, "But if someone else does, we're not responsible."

Irene's eyes lit up as she scurried away, no doubt to figure out how to get the most out of this latest chunk of gossip.

When they got to the car, Taylor muttered, "Unbelievable. Thanks, Ryan, for finding that out."

"Yeah," Logan added. "Now we can finally be rid of her."

"And we can end this stupid fake engagement," Taylor said in disgust.

Disgust? Is that how she really felt about this? Trying to find some way to delay the inevitable, Logan said, "But not immediately, right?" He glanced up at the rearview mirror to see Ryan watching him from the backseat and widened his eyes in a plea for help.

"Yeah," Ryan said. "It wouldn't look good for either of you if called it off right after Crystal left town and labelled you both liars."

Taylor frowned. "I guess. But we can at least make a plan for our break-up. And figure out how to tell our parents."

Not fun. Maybe getting rid of Crystal so soon wasn't such a good idea after all...

CHAPTER FOURTEEN

TWO DAYS LATER, Taylor sat restlessly in her living room, her stomach in knots, with Logan next to her on the couch. She carefully kept her distance from him as they waited for their parents. Ryan had left for the evening, the coward.

After they'd confirmed that Crystal had left town, Taylor had avoided Logan as much as possible, even going so far as staying with Amber one evening so she wouldn't need to see him. A freak snowstorm had helped as well, keeping her at Amber's place overnight. The only time she had talked to him, it had been by phone, so they could set the plan for their break-up.

Crystal had left town as promised, and though Logan had said he wouldn't mind continuing the fake engagement to save face, Taylor wanted it over and done with. She couldn't stand this deception any longer. It hurt too much, knowing he didn't feel the same way about her as she did about him. She wasn't even sure he was going to stay in Dogwood. He had nothing to hold him here after a couple of months. He'd probably take off and find another career somewhere else.

Her father came in and sat down in a chair across from them. "What's this all about?" he asked, looking back and forth between the two of them. "If you want to tell me you bought the golf course, I already heard."

"You did?" Taylor said in surprise.

Logan shrugged with a smile. "I hated seeing it so rundown, and Hal was wanting to retire, so I bought it."

Was that why he was shaking hands with Hal at the party?

"What are you going to do with it?" her father asked.

"After talking with Paul McPherson, I decided that what this town needs is something more like a country club."

Taylor frowned at him. "For this small town?"

"Hear me out. It's not about prestige. It's more about building a larger clubhouse, a place where the town can have parties, weddings...whatever they want. It will also help attract other golfers here to play in charity tournaments to benefit Sanctuary."

What a wonderful idea. "So, you're definitely staying on in Dogwood?"

"Yes. I'll need to, in order to run the business and be the resident pro."

She wasn't sure how she felt about that. Seeing him all the time when they would no longer be together? It would be painful, but wonderful for the town and Sanctuary.

"Congratulations," her father boomed, and rose to slap Logan on the back. "That's just what this town needs. But you didn't need to have a meeting to tell me that."

"That's not all we want to tell you," Logan said. "But we want to tell you and Mom at the same time. She should be here at any moment."

Sure enough, the doorbell rang then and Logan went to answer it. Logan led his mother to the living room, and

Sherry stopped to give Taylor a hug. "How's my future daughter-in-law?" she asked with relish.

Sherry had been so sweet to her, so welcoming, Taylor felt guilty about leading her on. She'd miss her when this was over. Tears threatened, and she couldn't trust herself to speak, so she just nodded wordlessly with a smile as fake as their engagement.

Sherry settled in the chair next to Taylor's father and gave them a questioning glance. "You have something to tell us? You found a venue for the wedding?"

Taylor winced and Logan squeezed her hand, gazing into her face with such compassion, she knew she'd lose it if they didn't get this over with soon. "You tell them," she said, her voice thick with unshed tears.

Logan took a deep breath, then said, "We're not really engaged. We just pretended to be so that Crystal would leave me alone."

Her father and his mother exchanged glances, calmer than Taylor had expected them to be. Sherry answered for both of them. "Yes, dear, we know. We've known all along."

What?

Logan seemed as stunned as she felt. "You knew?" he asked incredulously. "How?"

Yes, how? Had Ryan told them? If so, she was going to have one dead big brother.

Sherry shrugged. "You claimed to have a secret courtship under our nose. We knew it wasn't true, then when Crystal showed up..."

"Then it became obvious what you were doing," her father finished.

Her father, observant? She didn't think it was possible.

"Does everyone know?" Logan asked.

Sherry leaned over to pat him on the arm. "No, dear. Just the two of us, though I'm sure Ryan is in on it as well."

In the wake of this surprise, Taylor's tears dried up. "Why didn't you say anything?"

The two parents exchanged glances again. Sherry sighed. "Because we hoped if you gave it long enough, it would come true."

Her father cleared his throat, then said, "Have you two come to your senses yet? It's obvious you belong together."

Obvious to everyone but Logan, apparently. No, this was just her father's wishful thinking. He'd like nothing better than to have his favorite protégé a part of the family.

Taylor didn't even look at Logan, not wanting to see how he reacted to that statement. "It was just a...business arrangement," he said. "Taylor agreed to play the part of my fiancée to fool Crystal, and I agreed to help her get her business started."

Sherry shook her head sadly.

Logan continued. "So, we're planning a big fight and a public break-up. Don't worry, Coach. I'll make sure everyone thinks I'm the bad guy."

Her father frowned. "When and how are you going to do this?"

"We haven't decided yet," Taylor admitted. "We'll play it by ear."

"I have a suggestion for that," Sherry said. When they all looked at her expectantly, she added, "The Blossom Festival starts tomorrow. That's one of the times when couples can ask Match if they're right for each other. If Logan asks Match who his true love is, and Match doesn't respond, that would be grounds for a fight, wouldn't it?"

"You can't get more public than that," her father added.

It was obvious the two of them hoped Match would put them together. Though Taylor no longer had any such hopes, she nodded.

Logan looked pleased by the idea. "Good idea," he said.

So, tomorrow this charade would end. She felt happy that the pretending would be over, but that meant no more Logan, no more practice kisses....

THE NEXT DAY, Taylor and Logan joined their parents and Ryan at Memorial Park for the Blossom Festival. Though Taylor was dreading this, she had to admit the Renaissance theme was inspired, especially the gazebo that resembled a throne room. The weather had cooperated, too, making the day sunny and bright. That was spring in Colorado for you—one last hurrah of a snowstorm, followed by sunshine the next day that melted the slush as if it had never even happened.

Logan glanced down at her and held out his hand. "To keep up appearances," he murmured. "One last time?"

One last time before they had their big, public fight. One last time to be together as a couple. Though it hurt to do it, Taylor placed her hand in his and let him lead her through the festival, with its craft booths, games, and delicious food.

After they ate lunch, the loudspeaker came on. The mayor said, "Welcome to the Blossom Festival." He went on to explain the origins of the festival, then said what she had been dreading to hear. "And now it's time for all of our hopeful romantics to come forward to either get Match's blessing, or help you find your true love. Please, everyone, come to the throne room."

Logan glanced down at her. "It's time."

Her food suddenly congealed in her stomach like a rock. Time to break up with Logan...forever. She nodded and tried to give him a smile, but it didn't reach her face.

Logan squeezed her hand. "Don't worry. I won't let anyone think less of you."

They made their way to the "throne room" at the gazebo and their parents joined them there. Logan gave her hand one last squeeze and went to join the other hopefuls on the makeshift stage of the gazebo. Unfortunately, there was a big crowd around them. Everyone in town would soon know this was over.

Mayor Rutherford puffed up, loving nothing more than being the center of attention. "For those of you new to Dogwood, I'd like to explain the legend of our match-making dog. Following World War II when the country was rebuilding, our ancestors built this very park. The first Match was discovered when a young woman gave the dog a crown of flowers and asked him to take it to her one true love. Surprisingly, the dog took it to someone other than the young man she'd been seeing, but the dog was right, so they renamed him Match. And every dog bearing the heart-shaped mark since then has been renamed Match and brought soul mates together." He paused dramatically, then said, "Will Match please come to the stage?" Encouraged by her owner, Bliss McPherson, the black-and-white border collie mix leapt onto the stage and took her seat on the throne as if it had been made especially for her. Everyone laughed, and the mayor said, "I'd like to have the first supplicant, please."

Sherry gave her a hug. "Don't worry, sweetie. Everything will be just fine."

Taylor gave her a wan smile. No, it would never be fine again.

The first person to step up was a man she had never seen before. He stood with utter confidence and handed Match one of the crown of flowers sold at a nearby booth.

"Match, will you please take this to my one true love?" he asked.

Match took the circlet of flowers and headed unhesitatingly across the lawn to a woman who took the crown, squealed in delight, then ran and jumped in the man's arms. The crowd burst into applause--there was no doubt in anyone's mind that this was a true match.

Match jumped back up on the throne and waiting for the next supplicant. It was a young girl, maybe seventeen at most. She handed Match a flower crown and asked, "Who will be my true love?"

Instead of leaping off the throne, Match simply regarded the girl sadly and dropped the crown at her feet. The crowd groaned in sympathy, and the girl looked ready to burst into tears, but the Mayor kindly told her, "This doesn't necessarily mean your true love doesn't exist. He may not be here today, or the two of you might not be ready for a commitment yet."

The girl nodded, her head down, and turned into the embrace of a woman who must be her mother.

"And the third and final supplicant?" the mayor said.

Logan stepped forward and her heart sank. This was it. Soon, Match would out them as a fraud, they'd have their pretend fight, and never see each other again.

Logan glanced at her, then handed Match a beautiful flower crown made of Dogwood blossoms. "Match, will you please take this crown to the only woman I will ever love?"

Match took the crown in her mouth and Taylor tensed up, waiting for it to fall back in front of Logan's feet. But she didn't drop it. Instead, she leaped off the throne with the crown in her mouth and headed into the crowd.

No, no, no. This was worse than she'd even imagined. Not only was Taylor not Logan's true love, but there was someone in the crowd who was. Nausea churned in her stomach and she closed her eyes, not wanting to know who Match paired him with.

Her father hugged her. "Honey, I think that's for you."

"What?" She opened her eyes and saw Match staring at her, the crown in her mouth. "Me?" she asked incredulously.

Match shoved the crown in her hand, barked, then turned around and looked at her expectantly, as if to say, "Get with the program."

Dazed, she looked across the expanse at Logan. He didn't even look surprised. Just uncertain...maybe a little hopeful?

"Go to him," Sherry said, giving her a little push with a huge smile on her face.

Taylor took one step in his direction, and the crowd cheered.

The mayor took the mic again, saying something she didn't even hear. All she could see was Logan's face. They somehow made it across the space to each other, and Logan pulled her aside, behind the curtains framing the throne.

"There must be some mistake," Taylor said, searching his face for his reaction.

"No mistake," Logan assured her, taking her hands in his. "I love you, Taylor. I've been trying to tell you for days, but you didn't want anything to do with me."

Could it possibly be true? "But—"

"I was an idiot, thinking Ryan would disapprove, but he gave me his blessing. They say Match is never wrong. Give me a chance to prove to you that we do belong together."

He really meant it, she thought in wonder. Happiness surged through her and she put her arms around his neck. "No need. I've loved you forever."

He picked her up and swung her around, then kissed her softly and said, "So, there's no need to break off the engagement, right?"

"You still want to marry me?"

"I do." He dropped to one knee and fingered her engagement ring, gazing up at her with his heart in his eyes. "Will you marry me and make me the happiest man on earth? No more lies, no more subterfuge?"

Joy filled her completely. "Of course I will. It's all I ever wanted." She drew him back to his feet and gave him a teasing glance. "Does that mean we can practice some more?"

"No. No more practice. This is the real thing." So saying, he swept her into his arms and kissed her senseless. *Thank you, Match.*

DOGWOOD SERIES BOOKS

These are in order of publication, but may be read as stand-alones in any order.

Novels

Chasing Bliss, a Dogwood Romantic Comedy
by Jodi Anderson

Sit. Stay. Love., a Dogwood Romantic Comedy
by Pam McCutcheon

Love at First Bark, a Dogwood Sweet Romance
by Jude Willhoff

Must Love Dogs, a Dogwood Sweet Romance
by Karen Fox

Second Chance Ranch, a Dogwood Sweet Romance
by Sharon Silva

Her Fake Fiancé, a Dogwood Sweet Romance
by Karen Fox

Second Chance Cowboy, a Dogwood Sweet Romance
by Sharon Silva

The Ghost of Dogwood, a Dogwood Sweet Romance Short Story
by Laura Hayden

Fiancée for Hire, a Dogwood Sweet Romantic Comedy Novella
by Pam McCutcheon

Anthologies

A Match in Dogwood, a Dogwood Sweet Romance Prequel
anthology

A Dogwood Christmas, a Dogwood Sweet Romance anthology

Dogwood Secrets Unsealed, a Dogwood Sweet Romance anthology

ABOUT THE AUTHOR

 Pam McCutcheon is the award-winning author of romance novels ranging from fantasy, futuristic, paranormal, and time travel to contemporary romantic comedy. She also has fantasy short stories and two nonfiction how-to books for writers in print, and writes the Demon Underground New Adult urban fantasy series under the name Parker Blue.

After many years of working for the military as enlisted, officer, and civil service successively, she left her industrial engineering position to pursue her first love—a career as a writer. She lives in beautiful Colorado Springs with her rescue dog.

Contact her at:
www.pammc.com
pammc@pcisys.net

 facebook.com/Pam.McCutcheon.Author